Seeking AIDA

A. G. LOEW

SEEKING AIDA

'SEEKERS' BOOK ONE

A. G. LOEW

WARNINGS/TROPES

So…*warnings*.

Let me give you a brief run through of what you'll stumble upon (**skip now for surprise**):

- Daddy kink
- Double penetration
- Obsession/stalking (mentioned)
- Praise/light degradation
- Light MM content

This series was designed for those who crave that inner healing. Whether or not one finds it morally acceptable is an entirely different matter.

Remember, no judgement & stay safe.

To all the girls and guys blessed with an addiction to men old enough to be their father…

Samesies.

ONE

Aida

"**W**atch it, darling."

A man with greasy black hair and an even greasier smile holds out his arm to steady me as though he is a complete gentleman. Like he isn't the entire reason I almost fell flat on my ass in these sky-high heels.

His hip had bumped into me as I attempted to sidle past, no doubt intentional.

My shift is over, but I still have to be polite to the wasted men who come to my place of work with the intent of a hand job from someone who isn't their wife.

"Thanks," I smile, bull-shitting the gratitude through my teeth like I do so every damn day. Men like us placid and willing to serve, so here I am.

Maybe I can make a few quick bucks before I leave.

"You look pretty in red," he smirks, eyeing me up and down with panting need. "Very pretty, indeed."

I muster a fake giggle that churns my insides. "You're too kind," I gasp, tapping at his shoulder. The red-lace lingerie I have on doesn't reveal as much as some of the other girls, but it still doesn't hide a lot.

"Some of the other ones here are quite expensive. You're not like that, are you, gorgeous?"

Ah, there we are. He's not happy with the rates of the other women, so he's begging for scraps as if all of us don't hold ourselves to the same standard.

Better to let him down gently so he keeps

buying drinks from our bar, even if I know the 'tender isn't getting any tips from this guy.

"Sorry, handsome," I sigh, which isn't hard when I genuinely am exhausted. "I've just got off my shift. Someone else may be able to help," I lie before quickly sliding past him. I feel a grip attempt to wrap itself around my wrist before slipping easily when I walk away, as though they tried to make a last-minute attempt to stop me.

I don't look back. I simply weave through tables, chairs and drunk patrons before stopping to take a deep breath in the perfume-clouded changing rooms.

"Hey, girl!" Desirae calls out as she dabs some red powder to her cheeks. "Good night?"

I shrug, opening my locker to pull out my duffel bag. Truth is, it hasn't been a good night. None of my nights are good nights.

The cash I've earnt won't be enough—even added with my savings from this month—to cover my rent. My rent that was due three days ago.

And that's not even mentioning the rest of my bills.

"You?" I ask, because I'm not a complete asshole and do enjoy the company of the other girls. We're all just trying to get by, although Desirae does dabble in sugar babying, so she's been here less and less.

Good for her.

I'm sure most strip clubs are lovely to work in—but not mine. My manager sucks, half of the bouncers aren't bothered with what happens at their place of work, and the area in general is perilous and unsafe.

My colleagues are mostly okay though. The girls are all sweet and the bartenders are cool.

"Gerad's taking me out for dinner after my shift," she says excitedly. Although I can't see myself sugar babying, it does make me both jealous of Desirae and happy for her.

"I don't know how you do it," I laugh as I slip an oversized jumper down my body. "I'm exhausted after my shifts."

"That's because you haven't met the right man," she scoffs, like it's the most obvious thing in the world. "When you do, you'll never be tired."

I don't know if I believe that, but I don't necessarily enjoy my job much like she does, so maybe she has a point. That happiness must make you jumpy.

"So, you think he's the right one? And he's okay with you stripping?"

It's her turn to shrug this time. "It's been going well, and there's something more there. He's not too fussed, as long as he knows it's him that I'm coming home to."

I can't fault that.

I slip off my toe-pinching heels and tuck them into my locker with the few pairs I keep here—the few pairs I *own*—and replace them with a pair of block-heeled white thigh-high boots. They aren't necessarily sexy but comfortable, warm and easy to wear nonetheless.

Okay, maybe I find them a little sexy.

After waving off my jumpy colleague, I walk out with my hood up. I pass the back entrance and wave at Tom—one of the few bodyguards who I not only tolerate, but like.

"Alright, Aida?"

"Yeah, you?"

He nods, scanning the immediate area like he always does when I leave—checking for the threat of a lurking unfulfilled patron or jealous partner who blames me for their failing relationship. "Get home safe."

I nod and send him a flutter of my fingers.

That's exactly how the conversation goes. Every. Single. Time.

My social life isn't exactly anything to be proud of.

The walk home is uneventful—which is good. No more men try to grab up the small open space of skin on my leg, or whistle what they think is a compliment at me.

No, that's all well and good, but the front door of my small box-of-a-home being wide open and a bag of my things being thrown out of it isn't.

"What the fuck?" I cry, gripping tightly onto the shoulder-strap of my duffel bag as I dart forwards.

Roland, my not-so-forgiving landlord, charges out the front door with a face full of red. "You're out," he spits, folding his arm in the archway to my *home*.

Sure, it isn't very *home*-like, but it's mine. Or was mine, anyway. "What the fuck do you mean *out*?" I shout, trying my hardest to see past his shoulder, but he doesn't budge.

"You're never on time!" he scolds, and although it's fairly late at night, in this part of town, that's when most people are up and about. "I've given you chance after chance."

"It's only been three days!" I rip open the bag on my shoulder and fish around for my rolls of cash. With trembling hands, I begin to shove them towards him. "Please, *please*, Roland, I need this place. I can get the rest—"

"Stop," he sighs. "Just stop. Take your shit—" he kicks the bag of my things he chucked on the floor "—and leave."

"You can't just do this," I argue, trying to bide my time. I don't have anywhere to go. "Please, I'll—"

He ignores me as he reaches back and slams the door, locking it with his own key. "I still have stuff in there!"

He shakes his head. "No, *this* is all of it." He toes my bag again.

As I look down at the large duffel on the floor—a matching but bigger one than what's on my shoulder—my fight falls. He's right—it is all I own. All I own that's personal, that is.

Everything else belongs to Roland—furniture, cutlery, everything.

These two bags are all I have to show for the pain I've put myself through just to have a bed to lie on.

What am I supposed to do? Where do I go?

Roland drops the rolls of money I threw at

him in the bag—after deducting what is no doubt at least half of what I have. "There, I'll let you off with this." He raises and wiggles the cash he's taken.

At least he's leaving me *some*, but I don't even know if it's enough to cover a night at a hotel.

"Come back and I call the police," he warns as he walks past without an ounce of care, shoving the money into his jacket pockets.

People are looking at me through their windows or stopping on the other side of the street, but I simply can't find it in me to care.

Tears threaten to slip down my cheeks as my throat works, my chest and stomach hiccuping with forced-down sobs. I can't let these people see me like this—but where do I go?

I drop to my knees and start going through my bag. True to his word, he'd shoved all my belongings in here without a thought. Even *personal* items that make my skin crawl at the thought of him fishing through.

Menstrual pads, tampons—

My vibrator isn't in here.

I run up and try my key in the door…to no avail. He's already changed the locks whilst I was out.

Everything is in this bag. Even small, almost unnoticeable items like hair bands I know were left loose and lying around. But my vibrator— the most intimate item I own—is *missing*.

Did he see it and get nervous, throwing it away?

I think about the time when I first moved in, when he'd clearly eyed my ass and focused on my breasts rather than my eyes. When I was first late with my rent, and he 'jokingly' offered to sort it out with another kind of 'payment'.

I know what he's done must be some type of illegal, but in the area we live in, it's really not surprising and the police won't care.

I feel nauseous thinking that Roland's kept something so personal from me—it was one of the very few things I'd ever treated myself to.

It's not even like he's too scared to touch it—I keep it stored clean in a clear wrapper inside of the damn discrete box it comes in. He wouldn't even have *known* it was a vibrator unless he's purposely been shifting through my things.

My sadness turns to sickness and anger the more I think about it.

My knees scrape against the gritty floor as I bury my face in my hands. I have nowhere to go, no true friends to rely on.

In my smaller duffel bag are the contents I need to keep on me or use for work—my purse, some pieces of makeup, spare clothes, lingerie and heels.

In the bigger duffel are my clothes—although I don't have many because I hand wash most of them after they're worn so I don't need to buy more—including my underwear. *Gross, again.* A few trinkets I'd collected over the years, some small pieces of jewellery and…

Thank God.

Mr Jeffers—a ratty little bear toy that looks as though it's been through a war—is shoved at the very bottom of my bag. I sigh in relief as my fingers pass over the still almost-soft fur.

I'm so inside my own head that I don't register or hear the scuffling of feet behind me before someone speaks.

"Are you okay?" a deep, masculine voice asks. The voice is smooth and confident and immediately sets my nerves alight. Any man stopping to ask a woman crying on the street with her belongings littered around her can't be up to any good.

Or maybe that's what years of being surrounded by creepy men will do to you—ruin the species completely.

I cough awkwardly and wipe away my tears. "Yeah, yeah, I'm okay," I mutter, working to shove everything back into the bag.

I need to leave and find somewhere to stay.

"Hey," a second voice whispers comfortingly. A tentative pressure pushes down on my shoulder through the thin material of my hoodie.

I stop just as I'm about to throw my fist over my shoulder and turn from where I'm crouched, coming eye to eye with…

Damn.

My first thought should be *Leave me alone. I'm miserable and need to cry my heart out in a crappy motel room.*

Instead, my first thought is *Damn*. Because damn indeed.

The man crouched beside me has short, black hair, cropped neatly at the sides and longer at the top with a few small strands of silver. His face is clean shaven, and I can tell he's older—although incredibly handsome.

He's dressed in a suit that probably cost more than my rent—no, scratch that, it definitely does.

His eyes are bright blue and *seem* kind, but I've witnessed enough to not be trusting of any-one.

"Miss?" he asks, squeezing my arm. "Is

everything okay?"

I cough again. "I'm fine," I repeat, throwing myself out of that weird haze. I'm needy, is all. Desperate and lonely.

"You don't look fine," he says softly, and if someone else had said it, it may have seemed patronising, but from him it felt caring.

He stands, and holds his hand out, waiting patiently for me to accept. Something in my baulks at *not* accepting, so I slip my hand into his and enjoy the quick touch as he hauls me up before letting go.

It's then that I remember the second man—who's now stood before me, shoulder to shoulder with the first.

He's just as handsome, just as *tall*, even when I'm in my bulky heels. His salt-and-pepper hair seems slightly more aged than his friends, although still very sexy. His deep brown eyes also seem to be filled with concern.

They're both dressed in ridiculously fancy suits. "What's happened?" the second man—

with a voice slightly rougher than the first man's—asks, eyeing the bags behind me.

I'm embarrassed about how public my life is at this very moment.

My cheeks blush under their intense stare, trying to avoid eye contact. "I'm okay."

"Have you been kicked out?" the first man asks softly. I'm trying to understand why these two exceptionally sexy men care. "Where are my manners?" he chuckles. "My name's Clint. This is Ezra."

"Is that all you own?" the second man— *Ezra*—asks, repeatedly eyeing the bags.

And then I'm embarrassed again.

I think they catch it. "Hey, it's okay. We just want to help," Clint smiles. When I look back at Ezra, I realise there isn't judgement in his gaze, but worry, and maybe anger?

Just as I'm about to answer, a few drops of rain drip down to my forehead. Shit, if I'm stuck in the rain, I'll freeze to death. Not to mention my stuff will soak.

"Fuck," Ezra mutters.

"Do you have somewhere to stay? You can't stay here," Clint adds.

Obviously.

"I-I'll be fine."

Clint tuts, shaking his head. "No, we're not leaving you here." He grabs one of my bags up off of the floor as Ezra does the same to my other one. "Let us take you out for dinner."

I swallow, my heart racing as my head tries to catch up with what's happening.

"Dinner?" I manage to whisper.

"Dinner," Ezra confirms, so stoic.

"We need to get you out of this weather, and a nice meal will do you good," Clint smiles. "Our treat."

I have no idea what to do.

Surely this isn't happening.

Two super handsome men asking to take me out for dinner after I've just been kicked out of the only place I have to stay.

What the fuck do I say?

It's times like this where I wish there was something, *someone*, who would just guide me, explain to me what the right choice is.

I think about the past few years, about how hard I've worked for nothing. I think about how my only belongings are shoved in bags. I think about how little money I'm bringing in.

Does it really matter what happens to me anymore? It's not as though I'll be able to do anything to help myself.

It's an upsetting thought, but it's the one that solidifies my decision.

Anything to get me out of the rain and the street. Anything to put off the inevitable: homelessness. Anything to get a free meal.

"Okay," I breathe out, still slightly confused and taken aback by the situation.

Regardless of my own personal conundrum, I nod.

"I'll come."

TWO

Clint

"You must be freezing," I say as Ezra steps forward to take her other bag from me. Surely this can't be all of her belongings?

"I'm okay," she lies as she wraps her arms around herself. The rain is hitting us stronger now and soon her jumper will be soaked through.

"Here," I offer, slipping off my suit jacket. She makes no move to accept, still looking confused and bewildered. I hook it over her shoulders so it's at least shielding her.

It looks good on her.

Her faded pink hair—that we know she cut herself to her elbows last week—is already beginning to plaster to her face and neck, the straight strands becoming slightly frizzed.

Her long, black lashes are coated in water, and the wings of her eyeliner are starting to drip down her face.

She's only dressed in a pair of high, white boots and a long jumper—now with my jacket—allowing us only a small view of her beautiful full thighs.

She's spectacular.

She always has been.

We haven't been watching her for long. Only two years. But what better time to introduce her to the other side of the world, or, well, city? She doesn't have a home, barely any belongings to call her own—we'll change that.

I wanted to introduce ourselves sooner but Ezra wasn't sure. Well, now he is.

We just need to make sure she stays with us.

Ezra hangs behind us as we walk to our parked car down the street. Usually, we'd have a driver waiting for us, but we don't use one when watching Aida.

No one else is allowed to see what we do. We could deal with her particular profession when we knew she was returning home alone.

But now she's ours, and soon she'll know it.

No doubt she's confused as to what's even happening, our sweet girl. She's twenty-two and completely alone—not anymore. We just want to make her happy.

It's been long since Ezra and I have bothered caring about societal 'norms', and when we caught sight of our little minx, we threw them out the window. Who cares? She's ours, and we're hers.

"Where are we going?" she asks cautiously, like she's debating whether or not to follow us in the car.

She watches with a swallow as Ezra silently puts her bags into the passenger seat and walks around to the driver's side. It's not his fault he's a quiet guy—I think he's more worried about making her feel nervous with his slightly gruff presence—but he's not helping his case much.

"Just for dinner," I smile. "A nice place called Angelino's. Have you heard of it?"

We already know she has.

Her eyes go wide. "That's on the other side of town."

I nod. We'd been planning how we'd introduce ourselves step by step, coming to sweep her up now wasn't intended but necessary. We were going to wait a few more months at least, although we already knew we'd be taking her to Angelino's.

She's been before. With her father. Before he disappeared.

The point is to—hopefully—make her feel safer if she recognises the setting and holds a familiarity with it.

"Don't worry, you can leave whenever you'd like. We'll take you wherever you want to go." And that'll be our home.

Her eyes swim back and forth before she takes a deep breath, no doubt coming to her conclusion. She's so focused at work, never letting anyone see behind her mask, but she's already dropped it around us.

Good, because I love reading her face.

I bet she's coming with us because she's convinced herself there's nothing to lose. No, sweet girl, there's everything to gain.

I open the car door to the back seat and wait patiently for her. There's no rush.

But she doesn't make me wait long.

I slip in immediately after, keeping both of us to the door seats rather than dragging her to the middle—or my lap—like I want to. I know Ezra and I will need to pace ourselves.

Ezra doesn't say anything as he starts to drive off, but I know he's dying to hear her voice, watch her live, look after her. He needs her as badly as I do and she doesn't even know it yet.

She sits with her hands in her lap, fiddling

with her fingers and scanning the interior of our car. "Is everything okay?" I ask. I already know how she's feeling, but I want to put her at ease—and hear her voice.

"I'm just confused," she whispers. My sweet girl spends all her time catering to perverted men who don't see her as the woman she is, and I'm happy to see she's already dropping the seductress act.

My girl is sweet and a little shy at times.

"Why're you confused?" I reply with a smooth smile. Her cheeks and nose are slightly flushed from the rain.

"Well, you just— We're— Well—"

"Take a deep breath and use your words." I keep my tone soft, so she knows I'm not trying to patronise her, but soothe her.

My girl can also get defensive and snarky quickly—we quite enjoyed watching it happen from afar, but we'll make sure she gets the adequate punishment if she uses it on us. One she'll thoroughly enjoy.

23

I expect her to snap, but instead, she listens. I watch intently as her lips purse on an inhale and part on an exhale, entranced by her face.

"It's a lot." She's still whispering like she's maybe afraid. "I-I've just been kicked out, and now you two have randomly asked me for dinner."

"Is something wrong with that?" Fuck, I want to call her pet names and make her blush.

When she doesn't answer—and still doesn't meet my eyes—I place my hand to lean on the middle seat. "We think you're beautiful, and beautiful girls shouldn't be left alone on the street."

"You-you do this a lot?"

I can't help myself. I slide my hand under her chin, grasp lightly, and turn her face to look at me. Her eyes are wide and scanning my face nervously. "No," I say flatly. She needs to understand she's it for us. "We don't."

"Why me?"

Why you, baby? Because you're utter

perfection. Because when Ezra and I watched you dive in to help an elderly lady who's bag ripped open on the street, we became enamoured. Because you're beautiful.

"As I said, you shouldn't have been left outside like that. We want to make sure you're okay."

She swallows again—a nervous habit—and nods against my grip. "Is this a sex thing?" she bravely asks.

Do I want to have sex with you? Oh *baby*, I'd kill to spread your thick thighs and dive between your legs to taste how sweet you really are. To thumb your nipples whilst I make love to your cunt. To listen to the noises you make as our bodies smack together.

But no, it's not a sex thing. I would do anything just to be in her presence, to smell her beautiful scent, to have our ears blessed with her soft, smokey voice, to watch as her eyes widen with excitement—an expression we've seen only very rarely, but our favourite one.

It isn't just about sex. It's about how deeply we care for her, and how the only thing that matters is her happiness. I'd sacrifice sex if she asked me to—hell, I'd sacrifice anything.

We've already got a room made up for her. A few years ago, it was just a bare spare room that we'd never use. Already it's more decorated to fit my pink-haired girl's tastes, but we'll have to continue rendering it until she's happy.

"We just want to make sure you're okay." Not exactly a lie, just not the full truth.

Her eyes flick to where Ezra sits in front of her. "And him?"

Our eyes meet in the rear-view mirror—he's been watching her. "He wants the same."

She looks between us multiple times before I visibly see her body slightly relax. I haven't seen much of her sass—is my sweet girl tired? Has she given up now that the world has caught up to her?

We'll build her back up. We shouldn't have waited this long.

"Are you hungry, beautiful?" Her stomach rumbles loudly. We already know she hasn't eaten tonight—only an apple before her shift. She's losing weight recently, something we'll make sure to change.

She blushes slightly and I can see it now she's warmed up. Is it because she's embarrassed about being hungry, or because I called her beautiful?

"A little," she lies, as if it's something to be ashamed about. "Does *he* talk?"

I can't help but chuckle. "Yeah, he talks. Ezra, say hi." I know I shouldn't put him on the spot like that, he doesn't like it, but he needs to reassure our girl.

"Hi," he states roughly. "What's your name?"

Good call. I forgot to ask her, and she'd be confused as to why we already know it if I slip up.

"Aida."

We both repeat her name at the same time—

testing it on our lips for real this time—and she blushes even more. Sweet, sweet girl, how lovely you'll look blushing on our cocks.

"That's a beautiful name," I smile.

She smiles back, a little awkward but I don't care because it's her. We sit in silence for the rest of the drive, although I notice her looking at both Ezra and I from the corner of her eye multiple times on the ride over.

She's not exactly dressed for this kind of establishment, but anyone who has a problem with that can take a pole down their throat.

Ezra slips out first and hurries to her door before she can open it. She thanks him and I hop out after them.

As I lock the car, I see her eye it cautiously. She's thinking about her belongings.

"Anytime you wish for them, we'll retrieve them for you," I reassure, placing my hand on her lower back and using my other one to gesture to the door. Ezra holds it open for us, silently watching her.

"Sir," the waiter—Johnson—greets us like usual, eyeing Aida for a little too long.

We don't need to say anything. Aida is clearly confused as we begin to walk around the edge of the restaurant until we're in a private section.

The table usually only has two chairs—for Ezra and I—but Johnson retrieves a third one very swiftly.

Ezra pulls it out for her and slips my jacket off her shoulders, hanging it over the back of the chair. "Do you guys come here often?" she asks tentatively, pulling at the hem of her hoodie.

"Quite," Ezra states, sitting in the seat to her right. I slip into the one on her left so we are sitting facing her on the rounded table.

"What can I get for you to drink?" Johnson asks her, not needing to direct the question at us.

"Just water, please."

I have to hold back a tut of disapproval.

Treat yourself, baby, spend our money.

"Sparkling or still?"

I want to interrupt, to order her a gin and tonic like I know she likes, but I don't want her to feel smothered, or like we're trying to get her drunk. So I keep quiet.

"Still." He nods, smiles, and quickly retreats out of the room as Aida eyes it curiously. "How did you get this table?"

"We're regulars," I answer swiftly. "Do you know what you'd like to eat?"

She trails her index finger over the edge of the menu, unsure. "I don't really know what any of this is."

She wants her comfort food.

"That's okay." I take the menu from her. "What would *you* like?"

Her eyebrows furrow but she doesn't answer.

"Macaroni and cheese," Ezra grumbles quietly, noting her favourite food. Aida's back straightens. Ezra clears his throat and hurries to correct himself. "That's what I'm having."

I hide a snort. He *hates* the stuff.

"I don't think they have it," she states.

Ezra shrugs. "They'll do it." For us.

"That's settled then," I say with a big smile as I lean forward and entwine my hands. "Now, tell us about yourself, Aida."

She doesn't look as though she knows what to say. "There isn't much to know."

"Oh, I'd beg to differ." She's the most interesting woman alive. "Your evening looked quite interesting."

She blushes in embarrassment. Shit, I didn't mean to upset her. "I was kicked out."

"Why?" I ask, although I already know. Ezra had wanted to start leaving unnamed envelopes filled with money under her door when we first realised her situation, but we'd decided against it.

"Isn't it obvious?" She shrugs. "I couldn't afford it."

"So where were you planning to stay?"

"A hotel."

"For how long?"

31

She sighs, pushing away the fork she was playing with. "Look, why are you doing this?"

"Doing what?" I ask, feigning innocence as Ezra watches in silence.

"*This*." She splays her arms out. "Taking me to this restaurant. Asking me questions. You said it wasn't a sex thing, so what is it?"

Johnson walks back through with our drinks, placing Ezra and I's whisky in front of us. "And what can I get for you to eat?"

"These two will have macaroni and cheese," I say lightly, ignoring Ezra's glare from the corner of my eye. "I'll have the calamari."

He chews hesitantly at his bottom lip. He knows they don't have it on their menu—but he also knows not to disappoint us. Usually, I wouldn't be so pompous. I don't come from a rich background—I made myself one—but for Aida? Anything.

"Right away," he eventually sighs, picking up our menus and leaving us in privacy.

"It isn't a sex thing," Ezra confirms before

sipping on his glass. I do the same. "It's a you thing."

"What the hell does that mean?" She folds her arms under her breasts, her eyes hooded with a strong glare.

There she is. My fierce girl.

I have to hold back a chuckle as I envision tying her down to the bed, spreading her wide for me as I withhold her orgasm for hours until she's a panting, overstimulated, whining mess.

"And don't you think you're a little old for me?"

Then I really do chuckle. "Oh, little girl," Ezra basically growls, leaning towards her. "Didn't anyone tell you how much an older man could teach you?"

She huffs. "I wouldn't know," she mutters to herself, but we both catch it.

No, her negligent father didn't bother until her twenty-first birthday, when he took her to this exact restaurant, and begged for money she didn't have. He didn't return when he realised she wasn't lying.

"Is that what you want to do?" She raises an eyebrow slightly, twisting her body until she faces him directly. "You want to teach me?"

Can I detect a slight hint of flirting, or is she simply feeling the situation out?

There's a beat of silence as Ezra looks her over, scanning her face up close, memorising every detail, committing it to memory. "I think I need to."

She nibbles on her plump bottom lip, dragging us further into our depth where we want nothing but to surround her entirely.

"It's been a long time since either of us have been interested in a pretty girl," I admit, trying to get her to understand that we don't chase after women. Only her. "We saw him kicking you out, we couldn't leave you there. A warm meal and a place to stay will do you good."

"What are you saying?"

Ezra and I share a look. "Come. Stay with us."

She jerks her head back, her lips opening and shutting. Maybe that wasn't the best way to go about it? I have to remind myself that she does not see us in the same light we do her. She hasn't been watching and waiting, getting to know us from the corners of darkness.

No, she's shocked, and that's understandable. We just need to make her see.

"Who *are* you two? What's going on? Is this some sort of trade thing? Are you going to kidnap me?"

She's rambling, her eyes darting to the exit and then back to us. "Aida," I state firmly, laying my hand over the one she has placed on the table. She tenses underneath me, something I cannot wait to change.

"We have no intentions of hurting you," Ezra confirms, although it would come across better if he wasn't so stoic.

"You're free to leave when you want. To do as you wish," I add.

She waits a moment before taking a deep

breath and pulling her hand away. I immediately miss the warmth.

"So, you really just want to help me? And you expect nothing in return?" We both shake our heads. "How can I trust you? How do I know I'll be safe?"

"We'll show you," I say. "Our home has a security system—we'll put your handprint on it. We'll show you all the ways you'll not only be safe from us—but from others. We want to make sure you're okay, Aida, and we'll do as you wish to earn your trust."

She's breathing heavily now. "We understand this isn't exactly…normal. It's been a long time since we've cared for normal, Aida." Ezra states exactly what I was thinking.

"I need a moment. Toilets?" She stands and pushes the chair back, squeaking against the floor.

I point to the door that leads to the main restaurant, wanting her to understand she's free to leave. Her large heels—the only pair we know she owns outside work, the one thing we know she's treated herself to—click against the floor as she walks out like something's hot on her heels.

Please let us have convinced her enough.

I don't think Ezra is above abduction.

THREE

Aida

W*hat the fuck?*

    Okay, deep breaths.

I steady myself using the sink, thankful the bathroom is currently empty as I force myself to take shaking inhales of air.

My home was forced out from underneath me. Two hot, clearly very rich, older men approached me for some type of date. Said men have now asked me to stay with them.

Again, *what the fuck?*

I feel as though I'm dreaming, like

everything is surreal. Why would they want *me*?

Everything they said feels like a dream come true, hitting my heart strings perfectly.

Somebody wants me?

But what if they're dangerous? What if I'm being stupid just by being here?

I begin to think about everything. *Really* think about everything.

Here I am, standing in this exact bathroom, forcing myself to take deep breaths. A position I've been in precisely before, yet last time, I was here with my good-for-nothing father before he decided my lack of cash wasn't enough for *him*.

I've been alone for so long now. Every time things seem to feel like they may be settling, like I may have a chance of living a regular life, something comes and takes that away from me.

I've never been normal. That's clear to me, even clearer now. I like what these men are saying, promising me things that sound deeper than the words they're speaking.

What if I did go back with them? Would

they take their fill of a few days before leaving me back on the street?

Something tugs at me, telling me I'm wrong, but I worry.

How can they get me to trust them?

What they said—about societal norms—hit me harder than I'd expected. That's how I've always felt, like there was something *wrong* with me.

I feel a constant loneliness, and now I have nowhere to go, no money to take me anywhere.

I understand that at this moment, they're my only option. But it seems too good to be true.

When I arch my head up to stare into my own pale green eyes, resolution courses through me.

Take the chance. Take the fucking chance, Aida.

They could be serial killers for all I know, but what's the better option? Staying on the streets for the next few days, months, *years*?

No, if they are willing to offer me food and

warmth, I know I need to take it.

So with a straightened spine and raised shoulders, I strut out of the bathroom and back into the clearly *private* area of the restaurant.

The two of them are talking when I enter—and abruptly stop. They watch me with hunger in their eyes as I walk back to my seat. I've seen it in so many men—although never as handsome as these two—and identify it immediately. Usually, I'd ignore it, but I note how it makes me shiver pleasantly.

They don't speak as I lower myself into the seat, as though they're being wary of a rabid animal that could snap at any moment. Are they worried about how I'll respond?

"Are you okay?" Clint—who I've established as the kind, talkative one—asks, setting down his empty glass.

I nod, and inhale to take in the aroma of macaroni and cheese—which now sits in front of me. "I've made my decision."

I pick up my fork and scoop up some food,

blowing on it to cool it down. "And?" Ezra—the tentative, examining one—asks now, clearly eager for my answer with his harsh gaze, even if he tries to keep his body relaxed.

I bring the steaming food to my lips in order to test the temperature—holding back a smile as they both grow restless at my waiting game.

I'm happy I can eat my food without burning my mouth, so I do, and take my time chewing.

It certainly is delicious. I knew they didn't do this on the menu when Clint ordered it, but it tastes as though they do.

I can see Ezra's knee bouncing by the way the material of his jacket above his thigh creases and straightens repeatedly. Is he nervous?

"I'll come back with you." They both subtly release a breath I didn't know they'd been holding. "As long as you prove my safety."

"Of course," Clint says quickly. "Anything."

Sure, this may be super strange and super dangerous but suddenly I've lost it in me to care.

If this is what I'm offered, I'll take it.

It's certainly amusing to watch Ezra lift up his fork, take a sniff, try and hide a grimace before tentatively pushing it into his mouth. It's hard to hold back a snicker when he forces it down his throat with a suppressed shiver.

Slightly dramatic, but entertaining. I wonder how much longer I can play with his dislike for macaroni and cheese—maybe I'll request it for dinner.

"Enjoying your meal?" I ask, my question directed at both of them, but I'm more interested in Ezra's answer.

"Delicious," Clint smiles.

Ezra merely forces an, "Mmhm."

"So, tell us more about yourself, Aida." Clint's question seems to be an out for Ezra, who places his fork down to gulp at a refreshed glass of whisky.

"There really isn't much to know," I admit, twisting some melted cheese around my fork.

"Well, can we start with some questions?"

I nod. "Only if I get to ask some back."

His lips tip up in a smile that almost seems sly. "Of course, that's only fair." I wait patiently as he takes another sip, staring at me over the rim of the glass. "What do you do for a profession?"

"I'm an ecdysiast," I reply without hesitation or embarrassment and my head held high, but neither of them seem phased by that answer. I expected repulsion or enticement, but they merely seemed interested.

"Do you enjoy it?" I'm not prepared for Ezra's question, not when it's one I've asked myself many times.

Do I enjoy the confidence, the women I've met, and the act? Absolutely. Do I enjoy being seen as nothing but a sex toy, being preyed on by husbands whose wives are at home with the children, being targeted after work when a patron wants 'more'? No.

Sometimes, when I'm dancing, I imagine what it would be like for a man to sweep me away, to adore every part of me without their

base need being sex. I know it's not these two—
I still see the hunger in their eyes when they
watch me, and what other reason would they
have for wanting me? But it's only a dream, anyway.

"It has its perks," I manage to say. "What
about you?"

"We're the CEO's of Major and Bright."

Major and Bright…

Holy shit.

"Clinton Major and Ezra Bright?"

They both nod. "Did you guess that?" Clint
asks playfully.

I nod this time, silent out of pure bafflement.

These guys are *big* shit in Millstone Grove's
business industries, even *I* know that.

This explains a lot—no wonder we're in
such a private room—but also presses more
questions. Why would two men as socially large
as these two want anything to do with me?

My heart's beating a little quicker now
they've revealed themselves and there's

definitely more pressure than before. Do they realise their status affects me like that? They surely must do.

I shake my head and school myself. "I don't know much about what you do, but I know it's pretty big."

"Enough of that." Clint waves his hand. "We want to know about *you*. Have you lived in Hilltop Grove for long?"

"My whole life. I've never left North-Side."

Hilltop Grove consists of two 'Sides': South-Side and North-Side.

South was renovated when I was young and is now filled with rich people like Ezra and Clint and their business.

North, however, is the opposite. Both are separated by gangs, but North is known for its danger. It's where people like *me* live.

"You?"

"Born in North-Side," Ezra admits. "We moved here when we started developing in business."

"You two were both North-Side?" I question sceptically. "You don't seem the type."

"And you're saying you are?"

I shrug. "I'm not made for a place like South-Side."

"I don't think that's true," Clint says quietly, taking my hand in his. "I think you're made for anything. Don't you believe you deserve to be treated right, Aida? To be given anything you desire?"

He shouldn't be saying things like that. They pull at my chest and make it swell with emotion.

"I don't think I deserve that."

I feel pressure on my calf and realise it's Ezra's foot. "I think you deserve it all, doll," he whispers. "And we can give it to you."

They're only saying this because they want something out of me—something I'm sure I'll find out very soon.

Don't let yourself get attached, Aida. Men say all kinds of things in the heat of the moment. You *know* not to get attached.

"Is there anything else you'd like to know?" I ask, pulling my hand and leg away to sever the psychical contact and bring myself back down to earth.

"There is one thing." Clint places his knife and fork on his finished plate and uses a napkin to wipe his mouth. Both he and Ezra stand, Ezra doing up the buttons of his silky jacket. "Are you ready?"

That sounds like a loaded fucking question. Am I?

I stand, making sure my hoodie hasn't risen up and take Clint's jacket off the chair. They both move to stand either side of me, with their arms angled for me to take. Even in my thick heels, they're taller than me.

"Well?"

Without thinking too deep into it, I slip each of my arms through theirs so we are linked.

"I expect you to have ice cream in your freezer," I say as we leave.

"If that is what you wish for, that is what you'll have, Aida."

THE ENTIRE DRIVE TO THEIR HOME, MY leg is bouncing in anticipation. I have no idea what I'm walking into but I'm finding it hard to care.

It isn't a long drive—about fifteen minutes—before Ezra's driving us downwards to an underground garage that's filled with all different manners of expensive cars. The more I follow these two, the more out of place I feel.

Once again, Ezra opens the door for me like a gentleman and Clint grabs my bags, making no moves to pass them to me. "Are you okay?" Ezra asks as they walk me forward to an elevator.

I nod and smile, unsure of exactly what to say. Am I? I'm not so certain.

Clint presses his hand to an expensive

scanner type thing and it makes a beeping noise as it glows orange, then green. The elevator doors slide open.

"We have a highly secure system. We are the only ones with access to the building," Ezra says as we stand in the mirrored elevator. "You'll be protected."

"And if I decide I want to leave?"

The elevator stops, but the doors don't open. Clint types some numbers into a pad, and a moment later, they slide apart. "The code is 4851," he says without hesitation before ushering me out.

The doors close and I'm inside a fancy-as-fuck penthouse.

The walls are high, but there isn't much furniture. It's nice, and expensive, but it lacks warmth and colour.

Ezra turns and scans his hand before tapping something on the reader. It makes a constant beeping noise as it flashes white, on and off. "Here," Ezra says, lightly wrapping his fingers around my wrist.

The soft touch sets off shivers down my arm as I allow him to press my hand against the reader. He holds it there for ten seconds until it flashes green.

"Now you have the access you'd like. Although, if you wish to leave, permanently or just to visit somewhere, we recommend you tell us. We can have someone drive you or sort you out a place to stay."

I basically ignore Clint, letting his words sink in. They'd escort me places and find me somewhere to stay? It all sounds too good to be true.

"Would you like a tour?" Clint asks. Ezra keeps my bags on his shoulder like they weigh nothing as Clint presses a hand to the small of my back.

He shows me the kitchen, dining and living area—all of which are confined to the same open-plan room on one floor.

He proceeds to take me down a hallway with

Ezra on our trail.

"This is the bathroom, but all the bedrooms have an ensuite." It's like a crazy dream come true. There's a massive tub, a just-as-big shower, two sinks and a mirror that literally lights up.

They barely give me time to register what I'm seeing before I'm being ushered into a bedroom. "This one's mine," Clint says.

It's not as bare as the rest of the penthouse, with trinkets and personal belongings neatly spaced around. The bed is massive with black and grey sheets that match the walls, floor and pretty much everything else.

What catches my attention is the back wall—which is entirely made up of glass, presenting the most beautiful view of the city, glowing lights lining the streets.

They then show me Ezra's, and although it's very similar with furniture and the long, glass wall, his sheets are white and he has paintings above his bed.

The last room they show me is placed

directly between their two bedrooms. They refer to it as the spare bedroom. Already, I can tell it's a lot more homey than the other two.

The back wall—once again—is made of glass, like it follows the same window as the other two. Pressed against the wall is a massive, bigger than king-size bed, with sheets that have a black and white constellation print.

Somehow, this feels like another sign. I've always loved stars and watching them when it's a clear night, and now they're on the bedsheets I'll be sleeping in?

There's a rug by the bed, a bright pink one that matches my hair when it's been freshly dyed, which it hasn't been in some time. The walls are white rather than the dark grey that theirs is. The large wardrobe is mirrored, and the drawers are bare but they have a cloth over them like they're waiting to be decorated. A plush, light green chair sits in the corner of the room.

"This is where you'll be staying." As Ezra moves to put my bags down, a hefty book drops out and lands by his foot. He picks it up and turns it over to examine it.

I know exactly which book it is, it's the only one I own. My favourite romance that I re-read when times get shitty.

"A…*daddy dom romance novel*?" Clint questions, peering over Ezra's shoulder to look.

This time, I slightly blush.

The book is comforting, and hot, but I don't admit that to them. All I say is, "I like to read."

I do, a lot, but I never have the money—or time—to. This book was given to me by Desirae when we got drunk one time after a shift and I admitted some of my…*desires*. She said it was a good way to get it out of my system.

Neither of them make fun of me, or question it. Ezra just slips it back in the bag. "We under-stand this is a lot, Aida, and you must want to settle. There's products in the bathroom, clothes—all brand new—in the wardrobe."

"We'll be here tonight, but we've got to leave tomorrow morning. We'll be back in the afternoon. If there's anything else you need, let us know, or text us. We've left our numbers on the bedside table. You have free reign of the apartment."

They both stand by the door, watching me.

It feels like they're both putting way too much trust in me. Should I be looking at this in a different light? They've put me onto their security system, they're leaving me alone with free reign. Are they not worried *I* could do something to *them*?

I feel like voicing this but I don't want them to take away my handprint or lock me in the room. I may be taking a chance, but I still need to tread carefully.

"Thank you," is all I say before bending over to pull down the zipper of my boots. I slip the heavy material off and place them neatly to the side. My toes curl against the wooden floor, getting used to the new sensation of being without heels. I bounce back and forth.

My legs are now completely out and I'm

only in a pair of white ankle socks, but I don't feel nervous or exposed. I just feel…comfortable.

Fuck, thanks a lot dad for fucking off. I really shouldn't be this at ease around two men just because they're older and handsome as hell.

"We'll let you settle." They both take a step forward, and my knees go slightly shaky when Clint presses two fingers to the underside of my chin. "Sleep well, Aida."

They lean in simultaneously and press a soft, tender kiss to either one of my cheeks. "If you need anything," Ezra whispers, the sound soft and sensual in my ear, eliciting shivers down my neck. "Let us know, doll."

And with a squeeze on my bicep from Clint, they turn and leave. As the door shuts, the room suddenly feels all too cold. I don't like it, and I miss the warmth of their bodies near mine. It's not like the usual—sweaty, perverted men pushing against me with need. For once, I felt almost appreciated when they did that. Even though I know I shouldn't, because it's just my body yearning for that affection.

I run my hand over the door handle and let it sit on top of the lock. For some stupid reason, I back away before I turn it, and pick up my bags. I have to heave slightly, but Ezra acted as if they weighed nothing.

Would he be able to pick me up like that? My thighs aren't the smallest and my stomach not the flattest—not that I ever cared, my body is my body—but I can't help wondering how easily he'd be able to pick me up and sling me over his shoulder.

I drop them on the bed and immediately pull out the only thing I own from when I was younger. A scruffy, ratted old teddy with bits and pieces missing from the years that was apparently given to me by daddy dearest. I know, realistically, that it was probably from the hospital or some nurse that took pity on baby Aida, but it's stayed with me regardless.

I move the bags onto the floor and slip my

hoodie over my head, leaving me in the red-lace lingerie I wore when working. It's not comfortable, so I slip out of it and my socks so I'm naked.

The bed sheets are soft as I pull them back and immediately it feels like heaven when I settle onto the mattress that almost morphs itself to my body. For my entire life, I've always slept on what felt like a wooden slab. As a child, I'd layer up my quilt and use the old bedsheets as a cover—cold but comfier than nothing.

It's warm in the room—not too stuffy and not too breezy. Just right.

I bring the teddy close to my chest and tuck the head under my chin, really letting myself relax in these strangers' beds. But as I drift away, I just can't find it in me to care.

FOUR

Waking up to a soft bed with a glass of fresh water beside me and a note is very, very new and something that although I shouldn't, I know I want to get used to.

Morning doll,
We will be back around four. There's food
ready for you in the fridge, make sure you eat.

They're making sure I eat? Fuck, that makes my chest ache and my cunt wet. There's most likely something wrong with me—daddy issues, per-haps?—but after reading that novel about a girl who's taken in by a man double her age with a big dick and an even bigger urge to care for her every need, I've dreamed of it.

I push back the covers, stretch my muscles with a beautiful ache and hop out of bed with a spring in my step. The first thing I do is make the bed—I can't have these people thinking I'm a slob—and tuck my teddy under the pillows.

The ensuite has everything I need—even though Roland was gracious enough to chuck my bathroom crap into my bag—and I take ad-vantage of it. My products have never been up to this standard, I'd be an idiot not to.

They told me everything was brand new and that they haven't done this before, but they defi-nitely know a lot about feminine products—that's confirmed when I see the array of period products lined neatly in the drawer under the sink.

When I start using the products they

provided, I notice how everything feels like *me*. The shower products are my favourite scents, the period products are my brand, even the damn toothbrush looks almost identical to mine—but it's all *better* than I've ever had. Like more expensive versions of the things I use.

Maybe it's the irrational part of my mind trying to convince the rational part that me being here wasn't a stupid decision, maybe I'm looking too deep into this.

I push all thoughts away as I relish in these lavish products.

When I go to get changed, I'm about to dress myself in the clothes I already own instead of what is in the wardrobe until I see a box on the plush chair in the corner.

Another note is laid on top that simply says '*To Aida xx*'. I lift open the top and remove the white paper packaging. When I pull out the contents, I can't help but fall in love with the long, light blue dress that looks comfortable and soft—like loungewear—but also expensive. There's also a small, velvet box with a silver butterfly necklace and matching earrings. My breath is stolen at the sight.

It's not identical, but the small, pink butterfly tattoo on my v-line—the only one I have—feels psychical as I look at the necklace. *Another* weird fucking coincidence.

I hold the contents in my hands and look back at where my bag is on the floor.

To hell with it.

Without underwear, I slip the dress over my head and relish at how good it feels on my skin. The sleeves reach my elbows and the skirt reaches just below my knees. It's breezy and comfortable and I'm instantly in love.

The jewellery feels light on my skin and I twist the small butterfly gem between my fingers as I stare over myself in the mirror of the wardrobe.

I notice something different in the corner of my eye and walk over to the chest of drawers. There's a pile of three paperback books. The first one seems like a regular book, until I see 'Daddy Taboo' written at the bottom.

The other two have some varying words including daddy and taboo—and my cheeks instantly heat.

They'd seen my book when it dropped out of my bag and came in the night to leave me books like it, clothes and a glass of water.

Who *are* these guys?

My bare feet pad lightly against the wooden floor as I make my way out into the dark hallway where the natural light doesn't reach. I don't need to turn the lights on as it's a short walk back out into the main room where it's brightly lit.

True to their word, there is food ready made in the fridge alongside pretty much everything you'd find in a small shop, almost like they stacked it up before I came.

There are also a million different types of cereals and snacks, but I feel appreciative that they'd made me a proper breakfast, so I take it out and reheat it.

I don't feel comfortable taking my food to sit at the table, but I do anyway. It feels like I'm intruding even though they *asked* me here.

I do wish they hadn't left. It seems weird being here alone.

After I finish my food, I walk back to the bedroom and pick up one of the books they'd left me. At first, I think about how sweet it is that they've taken the time to do this.

But the deeper into the book I get, the wetter the spot between my legs becomes as I read the gut-tingling smut. It's exactly what I'm into.

Those *filthy* men. Do they have any idea what they've left me to read on their couch, or did they just see the kind of book I was reading and sought out more for me?

Eventually, I become too overwhelmed to carry on reading. The pressure inside of me is too much, but when I remember that my only decent source of relief was *stolen* by my dickhead landlord, I drop the book to the table and stand.

Sure, I could use my fingers, but once I

found the bliss of a toy, I struggled to go back.

Instead, I take my mind in a different direction. They said they'd be back at four—it's two.

I crack open the door leading to Clint's room and poke my head in, slightly surprised to find it unlocked. It's perfectly neat and tidy like I last saw it as if he never even slept there.

They've been kind, but I'm still nosey and unsure. So, I begin to look through his drawers. Papers, documents, even a pair of glasses—but nothing interesting. The rest of the room is exactly the same.

I then try Ezra's room, but this time, the handle is locked. I give it a good few shimmy's before giving up and retreating back to the living area.

There's not much left of my book, so now that I've calmed down, I continue reading. I get to a particular scene where the love interest is brushing the main character's hair, and he begins to stroke her neck lightly from behind. He grips her and not so long later, they're having heated passionate sex.

"Lucky," I mumble, putting down the book to open the next one.

 **EZRA**

CAN THIS MEETING GO ANY SLOWER? I'M dying to get back to our girl.

I wonder what she's doing right now. The only thing getting me through the day is imaging her laid back on my bed as she fucks her fingers and begs for me to come home.

Does she miss us? Does she want us home?

It's hard to not think of her so intently. It feels like we've known her for years. Well, we have, but from how we watched her, it feels like we've been *close* for years. Like her being at our home right now is normal, like imagining my cock sliding down her throat is normal.

To us, it is, but I can't imagine how strange

it must be for her.

"Mr Bright?"

I have to hold back an eye roll. These fuckers work for us, why can't they just do their jobs without needing confirmation from Clint and I every two seconds? If it wasn't for them, I'd be with Aida.

"Look," I say, eyeing the clock. Three thirty. We said we'd be back at four. I don't want our relationship to start off badly with lies, even if she doesn't care. Fuck, I hope she does. "What you're suggesting sounds good. Great, even. But I need you to…*stop*."

"Stop?" the young man asks with confusion.

Clint smiles at me as he leans back in the seat, no doubt letting me take the reins so he can daydream about our girl.

"Stop pestering us, bothering us, questioning yourself evcry five minutes. You have good ideas, and we've given you the reins to the department. We're busy men who don't like to be interrupted, as I'm sure you can understand, so you'll need to learn quickly how to do your job without leaning on us."

And with that lovely parting message, Clint and I stand, ending the meeting. We leave without another word.

"Thank fuck," my partner grumbles as we walk out the building. "I couldn't wait for that shit to be over."

Even though Clint's older than me—only 4 years older at 49—he's always been the kinder, less invasive one. He can hold his own, absolutely, and sometimes he can even scare me, but between the two of us, I'm the go to person to shut shit down.

"Me neither. I wonder what she's up to."

He gives me a knowing look as we settle into the back seat of our car. The driver nods at the both of us before shutting the partition.

"What?" I ask, feigning innocence.

"It's okay, I was thinking about how pretty she'd look spread on my bed, too."

"Fucking her fingers," I groan, settling into the seat. "Do you think she'll want to stay with us?"

I'm not used to showing vulnerability, but I know I can trust Clint. He's been my best friend since we were kids.

He sighs and leans his head against the seat, then turns to look at me. "I really fucking hope so."

The drive isn't long from our office to the penthouse, even though it feels like forever. By the time we're back, my mind is an anxious mess. What if she's changed her mind and she's not there when we return?

It wouldn't take long for me to find out if she's left by using the security system connected to my phone, but for some reason, I'd rather torture myself by waiting.

As soon as we're out, we dash up until the elevator doors are parting and a rush of breath leaves me at the beautiful sight.

My sweet doll is curled up on the couch in

the dress I chose for her, a book leaning on the arm rest under her head.

As soon as we'd seen what type of books our horny little girl had been reading, my cock grew so fucking hard I had to fuck my fist in the shower. No doubt Clint did the same, and he left and returned at three in the morning just so he could get her more.

We take a step forward and her head jerks up to look at us.

"You're back," she states, closing the book to sit up. I've been watching her long enough to know when she looks different.

Her cheeks are red, and so is her chest. The dress isn't overly low cut by any means, only revealing the slight top of her cleavage, but I can see enough to know she's flushed.

Then I catch sight of the books Clint received for her. Has my sweet girl been torturing herself? Reading these books and keeping her hands to herself?

I want to praise her for doing so well but

we're not there yet.

Soon, I hope.

"How's your day been?" Clint asks swiftly. It feels as though it's a normal day and we've come home to our woman. I can't wait until it feels natural like that.

"It's been okay," she says, her hands fiddling in her lap as Clint and I remove our jackets and hang them up. "And yours?"

"Yeah, not bad," he answers, lying through his teeth. It's been awful not having her by our side now that we have her in our home. "Is the dress comfortable?"

"Very." Good. I chose it because I know she likes light colours and prefers wearing soft, comfortable clothing when home. No wonder she does when she spends all day wearing uncomfortable little pieces for the enjoyment of other men.

I try not to get angry seeing her do her job. We both decided we wouldn't walk into her place of work because we weren't sure if we'd be able to handle actually seeing her with other men.

She's still sitting with hesitance, not as comfortable as before when we weren't here. That's okay, I understand why she's like that.

Clint moves to pour us a drink, and I school myself. I can be vulnerable around her. I *know* her—she won't hurt us.

"Can I cook for you?" I ask quietly as I sit on the other side of the couch.

She smiles and nods. "What are you going to cook?"

I think for a moment. As much as I want to make her happy, I can't stomach even another sniff of macaroni and cheese. "Would you like to choose?"

"Anything warm and homemade sounds good to me. Doesn't have to be fancy." I don't like that she craves for something so customary, something everyone deserves, but I *love* that I can be the one who gives it to her.

I nod but don't reply.

"Would you like something to drink, Aida?" Clint asks.

"Some lemonade, please?"

Clint pours her a glass—with ice because she likes her drinks cold—and hands it to her. I watch intently as their fingers graze each other's. Aida's breath hitches slightly. Clint looks even hungrier than before—for something other than food.

I leave them for my bedroom and have a quick shower, not wanting to be out of her presence for long. When I return with the intention to start cooking, I revel in the sight of her sitting on the couch beside Clint, both of whom look comfortable.

"Any man who can chuck a girl out onto the street without warning doesn't deserve to live comfortably," he spits, his anger clear, but Aida only shrugs, unphased.

I listen closely as I begin to prepare dinner.

"Eh, I was three days late on rent. I'm more upset that he went through my personal things and humiliated me. I swear, he even stole my fucking—" She cuts herself off with an aggravated sigh.

"Stole what?" Clint presses. "What the fuck did he steal from you?"

He pinches the wristband of an extremely expensive watch between his fingers, the gold edges slightly worn from the years it's been in his family. It's usually my main tell if something is amiss with him.

From the corner of my eye where I'm staring at her, I see Aida swallow before inching her head away from him, a rose blush tinting her cheeks. "My vibrator."

The knife I was using to cut vegetables with drops with a clatter against the countertop. "He *what*?"

They both turn to look at me, and my anger matches Clint's face. We should have looked deeper into her fucking creep landlord.

"Yeah," she mutters, pushing back into the couch pillows as though she's trying to hide

74

away. "I mean, he was always pretty weird, but I hadn't expected him to do *that*."

The fucking dirty prick is probably sniffing it as he jerks himself off. I want to wring his neck.

Clint—the pacifist he is—schools himself quickly and rests a reassuring hand on Aida's shoulder. "He's in the past now. Forget about him."

I certainly won't, but I'll make sure she does.

She nods, more to herself than Clint. "Is there anything else you need?" he asks, looking at her with obvious admiration.

"What do you mean 'anything else'? I haven't asked for anything."

"Well, you said your vibrator's been stolen. Therefore, you need a new one."

Her eyes widen and I chuckle under my breath.

We know you're not innocent, sweet doll.

"Y-you don't need to do that for me. You

don't need to get me anything else. This dress, the jewellery, the *books*. I don't need you buying me things."

Clint clicks his tongue and pushes away a loose strand of her hair. "Oh, sweet. But you deserve these things." She does, she really does. "Now drink up." He holds the glass out to her and watches as she drinks it. "Have you eaten today?"

She nods as she sets her glass down. "I had that breakfast. Thank you, by the way." She directs her thanks at me, like she already knows I'm the cook of the house. That's right, doll, I'll take care of you.

"That's it?" He clicks his tongue again. "You need to eat more, Aida."

She nibbles at her bottom lip. I can almost see the cogs in her brain turning as she thinks. "Okay," she eventually says, like she knows Clint means it.

"Good girl." Fuck, the blush that grows on her cheeks, the way her thighs rub together, makes me grow instantly hard against my joggers. If I move from behind this counter, she'll no doubt see the monster she's created.

I can't wait to feed her.

The room grows silent apart from the noises I make whilst cooking. Clint watches her as she reads her book.

Neither of us miss how heated her body gets. How aroused she no doubt is reading her filthy little fantasies. Fuck, my good girl needs a firm hand, a protector, and I'm going to give it to her.

When dinner's finally ready, I don't tell her straight away. No, not when I see her hips wriggle ever so slightly as her thighs rub together. I wait and watch, enjoying it immensely. As soon as she looks up to catch me staring, I straighten. "Dinner's ready."

She brightens and Clint holds his hand out to help her up. He doesn't let go as they walk across the room to the dining table. He pulls out her chair as I begin filling her a plate of homemade spaghetti and meatballs—another one of her favourites. One I can actually eat.

She sits in front of both of us so we can equally see her beauty. Okay, I'm sure it's so she can be aware of both of us, but I like being able to see her.

I *love* being able to see her as she eats *my* food, wearing the dress *I* chose for her, in *our* home. The only thing that could make this better would be to have her on my lap as I hold her hair back with one hand and feed her food between those plump lips with the other.

Pace yourself, Ezra.

"How was your day, Aida?" Clint asks again, watching her as intently as I do. She wraps her soft-looking hand around her fork and begins twisting spaghetti around it.

"It was…okay?" She shrugs. Is my darling doll not happy here? "I didn't do much other than read."

"Did you not enjoy that?" he asks. I hold my breath, waiting as she lifts the food to her mouth. She doesn't even realise my stare whilst she hums appreciatively around the mouthful.

"This is really good." Her voice is muffled, and she blushes with embarrassment and quickly covers her mouth as if she just realised she was speaking with her mouth full. Don't be embarrassed, doll.

"Thank you," I reply gruffly, shuffling in my seat. My cock is rock-hard watching her enjoy my food, caring for her.

"It's not that I didn't enjoy it," she admits after swallowing, quickly filling her fork again with eagerness I adore. "I'm just not used to letting myself relax with nothing hanging over my head."

Nothing will ever make her feel like that again if I have any say. Which I do. I worked hard my entire life just so I could.

"Did you enjoy the books?" he asks, no doubt wanting to hear how well he was looking after her, making sure she has what she wants.

Her blush deepens, and it's fucking beautiful. "Yeah," she whispers. "I did. Thank you."

It doesn't matter what she does for her day—or rather night—job, she's so much more than she lets on to her customers. Our girl blushing is rare because it means she isn't schooling herself like she does whilst working.

"I'll make sure to get you some more."

She's about to answer—no doubt in protest because she doesn't want us doting on her, something she'll soon change her mind about—but I interrupt, asking abruptly, "What's your favourite colour?"

She's taken aback for a moment before her expression morphs into one of thought. "Rose pink, for obvious reasons"—she points at her hair—"or sapphire."

She didn't say pink or blue, she answered true to herself like she cares about us knowing the real answer. Maybe she'll warm up quicker than I'd originally thought.

And I do need to know the answer for…reasons.

"Is there anything else you need or want?" I

ask, feeling the same persistent urge to care for her that I've been feeling for two years.

She shakes her head, obviously. "No, you two have already been so kind, and I'm still confused as to why. I really don't have any money, and I'm not comfortable with using sex as payment—"

"Aida," Clint warns with a low tone. *Fuck*, he's in just as deep as I am, and neither of us want her feeling like that. "We just want a chance. That's all."

"A chance for what?"

My best friend and I share a look. "We like you, Aida, a *lot*. We think you're breathtaking and we'd adore it if you gave us a chance to get to know you. I know it's not normal, and as fucking amazing as it would be to slide between those soft thighs and fuck you with my cock, understand that it runs so much deeper than that. We want a chance to start something real, to grow and maybe come out as more than friends."

My breath is held as we wait for her answer.

She's chewing on the inside of her lip. I want to devour her mouth with my own to make her stop.

"Both of you? Like…together?"

We hum our agreement. "If you're okay with that."

Please, please, please.

"So you want me to give you both a chance, as in, to *date*?"

"Whatever you want to call it," he responds. "We don't care for the labels because as we said, that's all from what society wants you to do. We brought you here because we want you, Aida, on a deeper level than friendship or sex. I'm not going to lie, or beat around the bush. We want you to one day be our other half. We want to see how this works. We want that chance."

She makes a face of thought again.

Please, please, please.

"It's Monday evening," she murmurs. "I don't have to be back to work until Friday evening at the latest."

Is she saying what I think she is?

"You have four days with me living in your home. Is that a good enough chance for you?"

Fuck. My breath comes out in a relieved rush.

"That's perfect."

Four days—three nights—to win this girl over and fuck if I'm not going to do every single thing I can to earn her.

FIVE

"M orning, sweet girl." Clint greets me with a smile as I walk out from the hallway. "Can I get you something to drink? Eat?"

"Some coffee would be great." Immediately, he slides a mug towards me with a proud nod. "Thank you. Where's Ezra?"

After we'd finished his lovely meal, they cleared up—outright refusing to let me help until Clint led me to the couch and lightly pushed me down—and I curled up to finish my book.

When they'd tidied the place, Ezra had said goodnight, placed a soft kiss on my knuckles, and retreated back to his bedroom. Clint sat with me a while until I fell asleep.

I woke up in the soft bed alone.

"He's got a few bits and pieces he needs to get done." Clint stands and urges me to sit on the bar stool by the island. "I want you to have something to eat."

He places a plate full of still-warm food in front of me and I can't help the way my mouth salivates at the smell coming off of the bacon.

"So, I was wondering if you'd like to go out with me today?"

I pause, the fork half-way to my mouth, and move my eyes to look at him from the side. "Go where?"

"I'd like to take you shopping so you can pick up whatever you'd like. Anything else you'd like to do, we can. You just have to ask, baby."

I swallow my food. "I don't want to spend any of your money," I admit quietly.

"Oh, sweet girl," he mumbles, turning the

stool so I'm facing him with his knees braced on the outside of mine. "We've got more than enough money, and even if we didn't, we'd want it all to go to you. I'm going to get ready, I want you waiting in thirty minutes."

I fold my arms and stand so I'm looking down at him—still only slightly. "You don't speak to me like that. If that's how you think this"—I gesture between us with a finger—"is going to work, then you're sorely mistaken."

His smile is lazy and boyish—despite his sharp, older features—as he takes me in. He doesn't need to stand to alter his presence and dominance.

"You're in complete control here, baby, but you also need a firm hand. You're too in your own head. I want you here, in the now with me. I don't want you overthinking—so I'm going to tell you how it's going to go."

He stands, placing a hand on either side of my waist, and the movement sends shocks straight to my cunt. "You're going to get ready, wear whatever you'd like, and leave with me to treat yourself. Do you understand?"

When I don't answer, he leans forward, traces a thumb over my cheek, and whispers, "Do you *understand*, sweet girl?"

I swallow again, this time from lack of saliva in my dry mouth. But then I find myself nodding, *wanting* to be instructed and told what to do, knowing I'm in complete control.

What if I asked him to bathe me? To brush my hair and get me dressed? Would he find that weird?

"I understand," I whisper back, and the smile I'm rewarded with is almost a perfect gift.

"Of course you do, my smart girl," he murmurs, staring into my eyes as he sweeps his thumb back and forth over my cheek. His praise immediately makes my skin feel hot and flushed, and it affects both my heart and cunt. "Thirty minutes, sweet. I can't wait any longer to see you."

And with that beautiful parting message, he

turns and leaves, giving me the perfect view of his pert ass in low-slung joggers.

I can't wait any longer to see you.

Fuck, these men know exactly how to make my body sing to them, know the exact right words to say—even if one of them isn't particularly outspoken.

I don't follow orders and commands—not even when I'm at work, regardless of a patron's fetishes. That's where I draw the line, but with Clint, it didn't feel like an order. It felt so much deeper, like it wrapped around my heart and attempted to burrow itself into the organ.

Lacking a decent parental figure is no doubt the reason I'm already falling for these guys—these older, smart and dominating guys.

But what I need is so much more. I don't just need to be dominated, I need them to know *their* place. To be so wanted no other woman can compare, to be so needed that they couldn't consider harming me in any way imaginable. To be cared for so deeply that my inner child can finally begin to heal—to feel *love*.

It runs so much deeper than sex or want, and that's why I've never found what I need.

Until now.

Could they possibly fit to that standard? To deal with my erratic mood changes where one moment, I'm a death-staring tiger, the next, a doe-eyed kitten in need of her fur brushing?

I'm getting my hopes up, I know that, but my steps feel lighter as I make my way back to my bedroom—no, their *spare* bedroom—and begin to go through the normal routine.

Doing my hair takes longer than usual because they've got all different types of products—like a *hairdryer*. Something so basic to most, but leisurely to me. At home, I'd just leave it to dry wet and brush it out before work. Luckily, my hair isn't too temperamental, and is used to that routine.

One thing I notice is how they have no makeup whatsoever. They have different face products—even the cheap face wash that I use.

It's random for them to have that when it doesn't match the rest of the collection.

Another weird coincidence.

After slipping into a set of blue lace lingerie—that Roland would have had to touch in order to shove carelessly into my bag—I decide against looking into the clothes they've offered me and slip into my mid-thigh reaching band hoodie and knee-high white block boots.

The same outfit I wore when they met me. It makes me feel comfortable.

I'm too nervous to look at the clothes they've stored for—*apparently*—me. What if they truly did belong to other women? My heart clenches at the thought of these men with others.

Not a typical reaction for me to have.

I use the makeup from my work bag and do my eyeliner, mascara and eyebrows, keeping it easy and basic.

Happy that I look presentable—albeit somewhat out of place beside these two men—I leave for the living space again, slipping my phone into the large pocket of my hoodie.

Clint is already waiting there with his arms crossed. His eyes narrow on me, and my heart beats rapidly at the sight.

I flick my eyes to the large clock above the television, and I swallow when I see I'm nearly fifteen minutes late. Why wouldn't he just have called and told me to hurry up?

He notices me noticing the clock and raises an eyebrow. "You're late."

I swallow, but the assurance in his voice is so fucking sexy. "I lost track of time." I refuse to cower in front of him just because he's hot.

I come to a stop, but he takes another step so we're barely inches apart. "I said thirty minutes, didn't I?"

My gaze narrows as I fold my arms. "Well, if you're such a prissy with time, why didn't you come and tell me to hurry the fuck up?"

In a flash, I'm spun and pressed up against the wall, his large body caging me in with a hand to either side of my head. I'm breathing unevenly, but I'm not scared. Not of him.

"Watch your tone with me, baby, because I'd *love* to see my handprints all over you."

"Is that why you didn't tell me to hurry?" I ask with a smokey voice that I usually have to force, but this one comes natural.

He hums his agreement. "That, and because I want you to take your time with yourself. You deserve it."

"How am I supposed to do that if you *punish* me for it?" I baulk, throwing my arms out by my sides.

"Because then not only do I get to see my girl refreshed and looking perfect, as she always does, but I get to paint her ass red, too."

Oh fuck, oh fuck, *oh fuck*.

So, he wants to see me treat myself, set me boundaries he knows I'll break, so he can punish me? The thought that he wants to care *and* punish me has my thighs rubbing together with need.

And he called me *his girl*. Sure, they'd slipped in pet names I didn't hate—no, I *loved*—

but this is different. A claim. A hot fucking claim I never knew I needed.

This is a big step. They've given me reassurance after reassurance, and although I don't want to pay them in sex, I sure as do want to fuck them.

"Although, it seems as though I've got some other things to punish you for," he mumbles, looking me over.

"What's that?" I breathe, wanting to know so I can make sure I do it again.

"You're not wearing any of the clothes we got you. Is there a reason you're hiding from us as to why not?"

I nibble on my bottom lip, thinking over whether I should be honest or not. What else have I got to lose? I'm already here with no home to call my own—I may as well stop giving any fucks and throw caution to the wind.

"I don't want to wear clothes other women have worn," I admit with a half-arsed shrug. I don't add that it makes everything feel cheapened and dirty, or that it shoots spikes of unreasonable jealousy through my body.

He hums, nodding his head like it's a valid reason whilst continuing to look down on me with pure want. "Those clothes have only been touched by Ezra and I, sweet girl. In fact, you want to know something even *better*?"

I gulp, and nod. Those clothes really were bought new for me?

"We've never had a woman in this building," he whispers, his breath soft against my nose. "You're the first, sweetness, and we want you to be the last."

He can't say things like that. They hit me too hard. He's only saying this because he's aroused, men spit anything in the heat of the moment they regret after.

But I'm the *first* woman in this building? I find it hard to believe, but I do. His face is so sincere, so adoring as he watches my features with a deadly sharp gaze.

"Come, I want to shower you with

everything you've dreamt of."

He takes my hand and pulls my gaping self along, my brain still attempting to catch up. He stops, and I wonder why he's just standing there, before I look up to see him already looking at me.

He raises his eyebrows and gives a pointed look at the handprint reader.

I understand immediately what he's saying and dart forward to press my hand against the scanner. It reads my skin before flashing green, and the doors slide open.

Clint smiles, presses a hand to my lower back, and gestures me inside. He's proving his word. When the doors slide shut, I remember the code he'd told me, and insert it into the touch-pad.

It works, and we're immediately moving. "I told you before—you're safe here, sweet girl. And we plan to make your dreams and desires come true."

Unlike last time—when Ezra had driven us—a driver is waiting for us in a black SUV.

Clint, a gentleman just as much as his business partner and roommate, opens the door and waits with a patient smile as I slip in. He joins me straight after and knocks twice on a small glass window ahead of us.

The engine starts and Clint relaxes into his seat. "Do you have any ideas as to where you'd like to go? Anything you want, baby. Clothes, food, new nail colours or something."

It doesn't matter how much money they have or how badly they want to spend it on me— I can't let someone waste money on me. It isn't even a pride thing as much as a trust and self-respect thing.

But, if he's offering, then I'll take a very, very, *very* miniscule portion of his money and buy some cheap necessities like underwear and such. Nothing expensive, just needed.

Should I ask for a new vibrator?

"Little sweet," he sighs, twisting a strand of my faded bright pink hair around his finger. "Our money is yours to spend. The more you take, the happier we'll be."

I don't respond—really, I can't with my current lack of brain functioning and confusion—so I settle into the rich leather seat and close my eyes.

Clint's hand never removes itself from my hair. I feel his gaze permanently fixated onto the side of my face. My skin prickles with awareness, but I keep my eyes firmly shut.

It's not until pressure connects with my thigh and I jerk in shock do I feel the tingle leave the side of my face. When I squint open one eye, I notice his hand is resting on my leg, and he's settled his own head back into the seat with his eyes shut and a small but blissful smile on his lips.

It's a gorgeous sight.

I don't know how long we're driving for— I'm too distracted to care, so apparently my self-preservation skills aren't what they once were— but eventually, we pull up to South-Side's biggest mall.

Filled with extravagant, expensive shops.

Fuck. This really isn't a place I'd ever even consider visiting if I was to pass through South-Side. Not that I ever would. It's rare that I leave North-Side at all.

I remember feeling a little sick when Ezra and Clint took me to Angelino's because of how expensive I knew it was—a place I'd been before with the man who ran off a long time ago. It wasn't a happy experience.

I'm beginning to feel slightly creeped with all these coincidences. Is this fate's way of telling me I made the right decision, or am I just going insane?

"Wait here," Clint instructs, before dashing out to come to my door, ever the gentleman. I smile as I hop out, arching my back in a stretch. "Is there anywhere you'd like to go first?"

He hooks an arm around my waist and pulls me in close, a possessive move that feels calming and reassuring. And hot.

Truth is, I don't know the shops around here,

let alone expensive brand names I never bothered to accustom myself with. I understood those types of things weren't for me and I quickly made my peace with that.

Clint no doubt senses my hesitation. "We can just take it shop by shop. No pressure, sweetness. If you see anything you'd like, let me know."

I give him an appreciative, awkward smile, thinking to myself about how I won't be asking for anything. Then I curse myself for not looking more through the clothes they offered me. Have they provided me with underwear?

I'm too embarrassed to ask such a personal question.

His strides—that I'm sure are usually much wider—match mine as we walk in sync. It's not overly busy but my social anxiety has always been worse in places like this.

At work, I'm a character. The patrons see something different to who I actually am. I play a confident— sometimes ditsy, depending on the customer—woman, who doesn't care about what's happening around her.

When I'm off work, it's different. I feel the passing gazes of strangers burn through my clothes and skin, judgement I'm no doubt imagining searing through my head. I can still assert that facade, but I don't enjoy doing it outside of work. I don't enjoy pretending. I want to be me.

"You're safe," he murmurs into my ear, like he knows exactly where my mind has got to. But that's impossible. As well as these two seem to know me, they're still practically strangers. I don't know much about them at all, even if it feels as though my soul has already been bared and discovered by them.

His arm squeezes my waist momentarily, bringing me back down to earth.

I may not know him well, but my body responds with a feeling of safety, and I allow myself to revel in it. I focus on the warm encasing of his arm, the press of his side into mine.

The first shop we see is filled with expensive

looking clothes. Clint immediately makes a move to take me in there.

"These really aren't my style," I protest. Sure, they're beautiful. And despite the fact they're incredibly expensive, it's true that they're not something I'd wear.

Or is it something I *would* wear but immediately discard because it's pricey?

I can't help but admire some of the items. A blue ankle-length dress with spaghetti straps covered in light sparkles catches my attention.

"Try it on," he says gently, bringing it down from the hook in my size. How does he know that so well?

He holds it out for me as I stare at it—bewildered. It's breathtaking, for sure, but when I go to read the price tag, it's tugged away from me.

He leans in close and whispers, "I'm going to watch you walk into that dressing room, try it on, and come out so I can see how radiant you look."

"Clint, it's nice of you, but—"

His arm around me is firm as he all but carries me to the changing room. The woman offers us a furrow of her brows with an almost amused tilt of her lips.

"Can I help you?"

"My girl here would like to try this on," he says suavely as he holds the dress out for me to take, the price tag now tucked into the material.

We both know I'll just look at it as soon as I'm in there, but I think he's more concerned with getting me inside.

"Of course," the woman smiles, handing me a card with the number one on it and showing me to the fancy dressing rooms.

Clint sits down on a plush seat directly in front of the curtain, the thin parting being the only thing keeping him from watching me undress.

"Let me know if you need anything," she smiles, but I'm entranced by the way he's looking at me. It's heated and oh so sexy.

I swallow, walk into the space and close the

curtain.

It really is a beautiful dress.

For the first time in my life, I keep my eyes averted from the price tag.

Just for now. Just so I can enjoy myself for a moment, entertain the idea of me wearing something like this.

Of course, the dress fits like it was made for me and feels like pure satin against my skin. It hugs me perfectly, the low dip of the neckline revealing a heavy amount of cleavage.

I can feel the tag against my back like a weight but ignore it burning into my skin. I straighten my back, suck in a breath, and let that confidence I wield so well wash over me.

I pull the curtain back. Clint immediately straightens as he watches me take a few steps forward. It's only us in this area, and it feels like time slows as he watches me.

At first, I can't tell what he's thinking.

But then his hand runs over his chin in that sexy, older man way as he lets out a deep groan.

It sends shivers over my skin and I can feel my panties dampening at the sound.

"Sweetness," he sighs, his voice gruff. "You look absolutely breathtaking." He stands and holds his hand out. I take it, afraid to use my voice in case I smash this moment.

He pulls me gently to the mirror and stands behind me. "You always look perfect, Aida, but don't you see? You were made to wear this, and I'll be damned if I let you walk out of here without it."

I meet his gaze in the mirror and suck in a shocked breath at the sight. He's staring at me with pure demand, warning me to disobey him.

And fuck, I really want to.

I want him to push my face against this mirror and pin my arms behind my back, one hand on my waist as he slips the dress over my ass and pounds into me with abandon.

My skin feels hotter than before, and when he leans in so his breath trickles over my ear, my knees almost give in.

"Or maybe you were made to wear nothing. Maybe your body is too perfect to be covered, too perfect to be anything but cherished. But I'm a selfish man when it comes to you, Aida. It may be your birthright to be waited on like the breathtaking woman you are, but the only doting you'll receive will be from the two of us."

His hand slips around my waist, up my stomach and over my breasts before resting around my throat. He doesn't squeeze or cut off my breath, he just rests it there, tight enough that I feel the pressure between my legs without even coming close to hurting me.

I want it tighter, so badly, but right now, it feels fucking amazing too.

He tugs me so my back presses flush against his chest and leans in, our eyes never disconnecting through the reflection. He holds me there and presses forward ever so slightly.

I can't help but gasp when I feel the hard pressure against my back. "That's right, sweet girl," he whispers, and I swear I see stars from that alone. "You feel what you're doing to me, what you do to every man? But do you know what the difference between us, and every man is?"

The only move I can make is a small shake of my head—I'm too entranced to do anything else.

"We know exactly what you need. We know how to make it feel unbelievably amazing, sweet girl, because we know *you*. You're ours, and you'll see how ruined you'll be for any other man."

He's only saying these things because it's hot, I know he doesn't actually mean them, but I don't care. I need it.

I lean against his chest so I press further into his rock-hard erection, adoring the way it feels. He groans in my ear. I feel myself gush at the sound.

"See?" He tucks a strand of hair behind my ear. "My perfect little girl knows exactly what to do with her tight body. She's so good, isn't she?"

When I don't answer, his gaze turns sharp and his hand tightens around my throat. "*Isn't she?*" he repeats, his words sounding menacing but sexy.

I whimper—fuck, it's a needy sound—and nod.

What the *hell* am I doing? I've never done anything like this before.

He feels my sudden change in demeanour and releases his hold. I immediately miss it, but Clinton Major truly isn't like other men. I expect him to move away, to leave my body feeling cold, but instead, he takes my hand into his with a soft grasp and kisses the side of my face, almost like a reassurance.

He knew my mind went elsewhere, but didn't pressure me, and made sure I was okay.

He massages my neck, even though his hold was never truly enough to hurt. "Are you okay, sweet?"

I blow out a breath but meet his eyes. He'd barely even done anything and it was still the hottest moment of my life. So, I nod, because fuck yeah I'm okay.

He smiles softly before arching back slightly to look round the corner. He must see what he wants because he calls out, "Excuse me, ma'am?"

A moment later, the worker from before walks into the current area we're in. Her eyebrows raise and she stops momentarily, no doubt surprised by our current position.

Clint's arm is still round my waist, his hand around my neck, and our bodies pressed tightly together.

Her surprise is only momentary before she smiles. And then I notice her cheeks grow pink.

Sure, it's nice to know how hot we look, but her gaze is on Clint. Jealousy rears her ugly head back in.

I feel Clint's body move as though he's silently chuckling against my back. He can't tell, can he?

His grip tightens. "Could you bring my girl

back some of your most beautiful items? I trust your judgement. Pink or blue are preferable."

My heart squeezes at not only the posses-siveness from him, but the fact he remembers my favourite colours.

Her hands fidget with her black pencil skirt as she nods and he informs her of my size. She doesn't meet my eyes once before darting out into the shop.

"Did you see how aroused she became watching us?" he whispers against my skin—which now burns hot with jealousy.

"Yup," I mutter, rolling my eyes. He once again tightens his hand around my neck.

"A jealous little thing, aren't you?" He presses a kiss to my cheek. "I'll allow that little eyeroll because fuck, sweetness, it's hot seeing you like that. But know this."

He uses the hand that was around my throat to put pressure on my back, pushing me down to bend at the waist. He follows, leaning over me with a dominance that has my knees weak and

I'm grateful for his hold on me.

"I'm obsessed with you, sweet girl, and the thought of any other woman makes me *sick*." How can he be so obsessed with me when it's only been two days? "But I *will* punish your disobedience. Ezra will be delighted to know what a naughty girl you've been, getting your pussy soaked in public like this."

"I'm not—"

"No?" he interrupts, the hand around my waist slowly snaking down my front. The tips of his fingers rest *just* above my pussy. "And if I was to slip this dress up, your little panties *wouldn't* be soaked through?"

He presses his hips against mine, grinding his hard cock into my ass. He groans—a low, untamed noise that has me gushing. "I bet you taste amazing, sweet girl. I bet your scent could turn a good man feral."

My frazzled mind begins to clear. "Are you a good man, Clint?"

Our eyes lock in the mirror. A sly smirk

takes place on his lips. "For you, Aida? I'll be the best man and the worst. I'll bring you so much pleasure laced with blissful pain you'll never want to leave my side." He presses his nose into the back of my head. "The smell of you has already turned me more than feral, sweet girl. It's made me *obsessed*."

I'm about to ask how he can say that but he's already pulling away and bringing me up with him. The worker walks out, her arms filled with different items of clothing—skirts, dresses, jackets. All in varying colours of blue and pink. She's carrying so much it looks like she might fall, but when she smiles at Clint, I know why.

Is she trying to fucking *impress* him by doting on his girl?

I scoff and fold my arms. It brings her gaze to mine. Her smile drops.

"Thank you," he says swiftly. "Hang them in there." He gestures to the dressing room I'd been in.

She nods, hangs them up, and darts out

without a glance at *either* of us. Good.

"I want to see them all, sweet girl," he says as he settles back into the seat he'd been sitting in previously.

My skin is hot and flushed, my heart racing. Has that all really happened? He'd completely turned from that kind, generous man into a needy dominant.

Instead of letting myself whimper under his stare, I steel my spine and fold my arms. "We'll see." And then I close the curtain, blocking his searing gaze from me.

My body relaxes but misses it immediately.

"Naughty girl," I hear him chuckle. The words make me lean back against the wall and blow out a breath.

I give myself a moment to calm down, trying to get the memo to my vagina, before slipping out the dress.

Because I'm a sucker for praise—especially from Clint—I do as he says and show him each different item of clothing the woman brought for me, ignoring the price tag on all of them.

Every single time I walk out, he uses his index finger to order a spin, and I do. And every single time I follow that order, he groans and nods his head.

He gives me different words of approval. "Beautiful," or, "Stunning."

But when I walk out in the smallest piece— a tiny pink minidress that reveals most of my skin—I watch with pride as his already heated gaze turns, in fact, feral.

"Take it off," he growls, darting up and stalking forward.

"What?" I sputter, stepping back. My heart starts racing at his sudden change in demeanour—but it's in excitement.

He backs me into the changing room and glares down at me. "Take it off," he repeats. "Or I'm going to bend you over and spread your tight little pussy in this dressing room like a slut for everyone to see."

My cunt spasms around nothing. I've never

been so fucking aroused.

I can feel the proof of it beginning to smudge around my inner thighs. I rub them together for friction but the slickness they're drenched in gives me no favours.

He groans and rubs a hand over his face. "I'm sorry," he murmurs before stepping backwards to stand outside the dressing room. "I'll be waiting out here."

He shuts the dressing room curtain. I'm left feeling horny beyond reason and *confused*.

What the fuck just happened?

SIX

Clint

Fuck, fuck, *fuck.*

What am I doing? Putting pressure on Aida like that is wrong, she needs time to understand what's happening.

But she just looked so *needy*, so *wanton*. It's the sexiest fucking thing I've ever seen.

She's perfection, but I know rushing into things isn't right. I don't want her thinking we're only here for sex, because as badly as I *do* want to impale her on my cock, I want to care for her and love her.

I wait patiently for her to undress. My heart wrenches as she slides the curtain to the side, her face a mix of weariness and sadness.

I didn't mean to make her feel like that. Fuck, did she think I was rejecting her? We can't have that.

With practice that I've been using ever since I started growing our business, I regain myself and push the thoughts from my cock aside.

I smile and offer my hand. She gives the appendage a confused look before tentatively taking it. "You like them all?"

She looks back into the changing room where the clothes are waiting. "They're lovely, really, but I can't spend your money like that."

I chuckle and pull her into my side. I walk her out into the main shop where I see the same woman from before. She immediately brightens and looks towards me.

Pretty disrespectful when I'd been basically dry humping Aida in the changing rooms and making sure this woman *knew* I was taken.

"Is everything okay?" she asks, so willing to please, but it just makes me feel a little ill. I look down at Aida at my side. The thought of *her* so willing to please, but also so willing for punishment, instantly cures my sickness and more blood rushes south.

"Ring up every item left in the dressing room," I demand without a smile. She was clearly ignoring Aida which makes it very hard to be kind.

She's about to say something, probably, 'Absolutely, sir, right away!' but I pull Aida with me in the direction of the tills.

"*What*?" she spits in a low hiss, looking at the other shoppers around us as if they're judging her. A woman *does* offer her outfit a curious look—but that's all. My girl is too in her own head. "No, that's too much, Clint."

I can only laugh. "Only the best for you, Aida. Now, is there anything else you'd like? Some sleepwear, or to get your hair done?"

She looks at me as though I'm crazy then shakes her head as her mouth opens and closes in shock.

"Ah, you need some comfy clothes. I know you like those."

I turn and give a smile to our server as she turns the reader towards me. I look back at my girl, her eyes fixated on mine, as I tap the machine with my card.

It's like foreplay. Her gaze doesn't leave mine as it beeps with confirmation, or as I slip my card into my back pocket—almost as if we're challenging each other.

As soon as her clothes are bagged, I slip them onto my arm and wrap the other around her waist. Without a second glance at our leering friend, we leave the store.

"So, where to now, sweet girl?"

She stops me in my tracks and spins to face me, her pastel pink hair flowing out. "Nowhere!" she snaps, her arms folding beneath her breasts. "Clint, you can't—"

"*Aida,* I *can*," I smirk, adoring the way her chest heaves in anger.

"No, it's not— It's too— There's not— *Ugh*!" She throws her arms out in frustration. I chuckle at the sight of my little Aida growing angrier by the moment.

"Come," I instruct, gripping her hand in mine. "If you're not going to tell me what you want, I'll tell you what I *know* you want."

She offers me a pointed look with raised brows, but there's curiosity there as well. Like she wants to see how well I know her.

So well, little sweet.

"Well, I know you prefer comfort over style, so we'll go crazy on that. You've been playing with the ends of your hair and examining them— you want a trim. And you've been eyeing your roots in the mirror—you want a re-dye. I'm guessing we haven't supplied you with *every-thing* you want and need, as much as we tried to, so there'll be a few bits and bobs you want to pick up as well."

She gapes up at me and almost stumbles. "Careful," I taunt, adoring the way her plump lips stay apart.

"Clint, seriously, I don't need all this stuff."

"No, baby, of course you don't. But you *deserve* it, that's the difference."

We keep walking through the shopping centre until I'm pulling her into a shop that looks filled with comfortable wear.

She doesn't even meet my eyes as I throw different variations of t-shirts, jackets, hoodies, joggers and shorts into a basket.

"Cheer up, baby," I sigh as we leave the shop. I want to get her hair done and such if she wants it but seeing her like this—so distant—is breaking my heart.

I lead her back outside and towards our SUV. After I've placed all the bags into the boot, I turn to face her.

She folds her arms and looks away with the most adorable slight jutting out of her bottom lip. "Aw, what's that face for?"

"You shouldn't be doing this for me, Clint. I-I don't know why you are, but I don't deserve it."

My heart can't help wrenching at my girl's words—she truly believes what she says.

"Look at me, Aida."

When she doesn't make a move to look at me, I softly grasp her jaw and turn her to face me.

Her light green eyes slowly move up to meet my intense gaze, and when she does, I almost crumble at the sight. My girl is staring up at me with doe-eyes and glistening lips from constant nibbling, looking like a wet dream, but knowing it's with sadness immediately douses out those thoughts.

"I know you don't see what we do, but what we see is perfection. We see this strong, young woman who needs a fucking break, and we want to be the ones to gift you everything your heart desires. The thought of another man doing what we want to do—what I'm *trying* to do—makes me feel sick."

I watch as her head lifts up ever so slightly, like my words are *finally* getting through to her.

"Let us look after you baby. You promised us four days, let us win you over in those four days. This money? It means nothing to us. But caring for you? Absolutely everything."

When I see her shoulders slump slightly, releasing their tension, I can't help the stutter that goes through my heart and the breath I let out in relief.

She holds my gaze, but after a pause, nods. "Okay," she whispers. "But I have a question."

"Anything, baby. Ask us anything you'd like."

She nibbles her bottom lip—I have to force myself to not grip her wrists and punish her for the action that no doubt is causing her pain and leaving them red and swollen—as she eyes the boot of the car.

"I get the sexy clothes, but why the comfortable ones? Wouldn't you rather I resort to wearing something revealing over practical?"

Her words are like a sharp stab to the chest, but the pain dulls as I remind myself that she's new, she doesn't understand the way Ezra and I feel for her—it's not her fault she'd make an assumption that, for any other man, would most likely be true. Especially not after the cards she's been dealt over the years.

No, she just doesn't understand yet, and that's okay. "Those 'sexy' clothes? They're to make *you* feel good, baby. Wear them when you're alone, in front of us—I don't care, just wear what makes you happy. You look just as fucking sexy in sweats, and I'd much rather you wear them if that's what you'd prefer."

I can't let her dwell on my words—she's still wrapping her head around things—so I twist a chunk of her hair around my finger. "You want your hair done, baby?"

There's a war in her mind reflecting through her eyes but I adore watching as she makes her decision. Her curls bounce up and down as she nods. It's so fucking cute, and insanely sexy.

That's it, baby. Let daddy take care of you.

It's not the first time I've thought about her using that name for me and it certainly won't be the last. Before her, Ezra and I had never understood the urge, but after a year of obsessing over her, we both confided in each other about it.

My driver hasn't returned yet because I've not sent him the text to, so I know there's no confusion as we walk away. We don't go back into the main centre but walk along the streets until we find a hair salon.

It doesn't take long and I'm disappointed we find one so soon because she releases my hand when I step forward to open the door for her.

We're immediately greeted by a bubbly woman with a green and white mohawk. "Afternoon, guys! What can I do for you today?"

Aida nuzzles slightly into my side and looks up at me with those doe-eyes once again. My sweet, shy girl wants me to speak for her? To arrange her appointments?

Fuck, my cock is so hard.

"My girl here would like to have her hair trimmed and recoloured." The workers' eyes widen ever so slightly as they flick between us. I wonder what she's thinking, she probably assumed I was her father. "Do you have space?"

She swallows and recovers quickly. "Absolutely," she beams, a bright smile on her face as she flicks through a book on a podium. "I'll just take your name, phone number and run you through the different services we're offering."

I do the speaking for Aida, letting her answer the questions I can't. Every time one crops up, like what her mobile number is or if she'd like a certain treatment involved, she looks up at me expectantly. I nod and she answers the worker.

It's so enticing watching her rely on me, waiting for my permission to answer.

I'm going to praise her beautiful body when we're home.

The worker—LeeAnne—takes Aida over to a free chair and introduces her to the woman who'll be doing her hair. I sit on the closest seat to her in the waiting area—directly behind her.

Nobody warned me how long it would take, and by the time she's finished, my eyes are fluttering shut. I jerk awake when a soft giggle reaches my ears.

"All done?" I murmur, forcing myself to stand on jelly legs. Her hair is brighter than before, her curls fresh and filled with volume. "Wow, baby, you look stunning."

She beams at my compliment and the sight of her preening beneath me makes my gaze hazy with lust.

I rush her to pay, and she still seems uneasy as I use my card, but I can tell her stride is a little lighter as we leave the salon.

I'm pulling her along the street quickly. I want to take her to get her nails done or have someone plaster pasty shit on her face whilst they play relaxing music, but I *need* to have some sort of intimate connection with her—*fuck*, even just a hug.

126

"Clint?" she questions as I drag her to the SUV. I send a message to my driver and practically carry Aida into the back seat, shutting the door behind me.

He'll be here soon but I need her on me right now. He won't be able to hear or see anything with the partition regardless.

I sit myself in the middle seat and move her to sit sideways on my lap so her legs hang over mine. "Is this okay?" I whisper, trailing my lips up her throat.

I adore the way she shivers against me, and the muffled, "Mmhm," she gives me as confirmation that goes straight to my cock.

I press my nose into the crook of her neck and inhale, my hand wrapping around her waist to keep her still. She breathes out, and my head begins to feel full from her intoxicating smell alone.

She's not sitting on my cock—more on my thighs—and as badly as I want to feel the pressure of her round ass against me, I know we've already taken a massive step today, and that alone has me smiling like a crazed man and practically on the verge of coming in my pants.

I breathe out against her skin and adore the goosebumps I elicit. "Thank you for letting me take care of you today, baby. I'm so proud of you."

She leans her head back to give me more access and whimpers, her hips slightly shifting as though my words have turned her on.

That's it, baby. I know what you want, what you *need.*

She continues to move her hips, grinding against air. She's a needy little thing and I want to give her what she desires.

It isn't about me; I just want to give myself over to her completely.

"You look so beautiful, sweet," I praise, sliding one hand over her thigh and the other to the back of her neck. "That's it," I whisper, slipping under her jumper to bunch it around her waist. I cup her cunt over her panties, pushing pressure over the space and holding still.

She gasps and stops. "Use my hand, baby. Use *me*, make yourself come."

She swallows and blinks at me, no doubt coming down from her hazy lust to war with herself. I can't have that now, can I?

"Do you want to be a good girl for me? Earn my words and praise? Grind against me, baby. Let me feel how soaked your panties can get."

My words snap her into action. She grabs my shirt as she pushes her hips forward against my palm. Her mouth opens on a breath and her eyes shut as she leans her head back.

It's the most beautiful sight.

"Good girl, good fucking girl." The car is full of the sounds of her moans and pants and whimpers as she works herself over on my hand like it's her personal fuck-toy.

If that's what she needs, then that's what I'll be.

"Does it feel good, sweet?" Her panties are already drenched with her slick and coating my skin. I want to bring my hand to my mouth and jerk my cock as I lap at the liquid. "Does daddy's hand on your cunt feel good?"

"Yes—oh, *fuck*!" she cries, her grip becoming death-like on my shirt as she rocks faster and faster, grinding without thought. She's chasing her orgasm and doesn't care about the rest of the world around her.

I cup her harder, adding more pressure, and her legs begin to shake. "I asked you a question," I spit, gripping the back of her neck tighter and angling my palm so I can add extra pressure to her clit.

"Yes!" she gasps, and I use my hold on the back of her head to force her to face me. Her pastel green eyes are stunning beneath hooded lids. She looks blissed out, and if she was any closer to my cock, I'd be dry humping her back like a starved man. It would take me less than ten seconds to come staring at the sight before me, not that I'd ever let that happen. "So, so good. Don't stop. Don't stop. I'm close, I'm—"

"Come, *now*. Come for daddy," I order, my lips skimming across hers, and she does.

Oh fuck, she does.

Her eyes roll, almost crossing, and soft thighs clamp my hand tightly between her legs, not letting me go. Her hips shake in erratic, harsh thrusts as she works herself through the orgasm, the sight almost feral as she gives no fucks and humps my hand.

I have to clamp my teeth so I don't follow her right over that edge.

I feel the moment it becomes too much, and she quickly opens her legs to push me away. I let her—I know it's not because she wants me away, but because her skin is so sensitive her cunt is no doubt throbbing right now.

We've seen how receptive she is to touch, even innocent touch like a brush of an arm against hers. She'd notice it like it was stronger than you'd think the pressure was. It didn't take long to figure out how delicate her skin was with all the products she bought solely for 'sensitive skin'.

She whimpers and slows her thrusts as she comes down from her orgasmic high. "Good girl," I coo, brushing her hair away from her face.

"Daddy's proud of you."

SEVEN

Aida

*D*addy's proud of you.

I try to stifle a moan as I think about what we just did, the driver now taking us back to the penthouse whilst Clint and I sit next to each other like nothing ever happened.

His large hand is spread over my leg, his thick fingers twitching every now and again against my inner thigh as if to remind me that he's there—that he brought me to a feral orgasm with nothing but his words. I did all the rest—me. It's dominating and commanding and I adore it.

It's like he can't help touching me, like he needs constant connection between our bodies.

It's silent as we make our way back, but not awkward like it once was. No, now it's more comfortable, and when I flick my eyes over for a glance that lasts less than a second—one I've done multiple times throughout the drive—I still see a small, blissed out smile on his lips as he stares down at where we connect.

I always knew I had a thing for the whole *daddy* idea, but it'd never been made a reality. And now it has, I'm obsessed. I need more, I can't just have a taste and forget about it.

What I said about this not being a sex thing? Forget about it. Throw it out the window or shove it down the drain. Annihilate the idea with a mix of explosives.

But at the same time, it's so much more than a sex thing. It—to me—feeds my inner child and my past self who need healing. It weaves its way through my heart and under my skin like a protective barrier, making me feel safe from the world.

I know it doesn't mean the same to Clint, but until our time is up and I'm thrown back into the grasp of reality, I'm going to pretend it does. Maybe then I'll be able to leave this lifestyle— that I oh-so-badly want to get used to—with hope and determination.

After we park in the underground lot beneath their penthouse—one that's fucking impressive now I've gone out of my way to watch it as we pass by—Clint's phone buzzes in his pocket.

He reads whatever it is he received, and a moment later, he's smiling directly at me before leaving me confused and rushing round to open the door for me.

Why is he suddenly so happy?

Did a woman text him?

That thought brings up ugly emotions that wrench at my chest. I shouldn't be feeling that way over him when all we've really shared is a lusted up, one-sided orgasm.

Besides, I'm an erotic dancer, I shouldn't be getting attached to him when I know my *skills* are the only reason men want me around.

It's now that I realise how little time I've spent thinking about work and returning, being so distracted by everything else around me. In fact, since coming here, I don't think I've thought about it once.

But now it's in my head as Clint presses a hand to my lower back—his favourite place to hold me as we walk, apparently—and we walk together towards the elevator.

Doors shut, and we're riding silently up to the top.

I've always been a dancer, but throughout my life, it's never been out of desire to do it, and more out of convenience.

Growing up, my father didn't care what I did, and my mother was more worried about who she could get to care for me for free so she could spend more time with people who weren't daddy dearest.

A kids club in walking distance—so, an hour away on my little kid's legs late at night without anyone to pick me up—started to hold free dance lessons three times a week.

To my mother, that was three nights she had sorted out to score some sex or drugs. To little Aida, it was a big social event and I looked forward to getting out of the house.

I was a natural at dancing and found myself growing close to my dance teacher—a kind, young woman with bright pink hair.

She was always so generous. She'd bring extras of her snacks so I could have some and another bottle of water so I wouldn't get thirsty. She paid—or 'invested in' as she'd called it so I wouldn't feel bad—for my new dance clothes and appropriate footwear.

I stuck to the lessons for years until it was time for me to leave high school. Then, dad had left completely, and my mother's soul didn't exist in her body.

It wasn't long after that she'd died.

I was left with no money, no house, no nothing. So, I turned to the only person I could—my dance teacher. But instead of finding her to talk, I found her practising with her friends—her stripper friends.

She wasn't embarrassed, and explained what she did for a living aside from giving free dance lessons to the local youth.

She didn't tell me where she worked—I wouldn't have asked anyway because I was trying to distance myself from the attachment I had towards her—but I did some digging and found a place hiring.

I'd been using the last few scraps from the cookie jar on cheap hotel rooms, so it was the only option I really had.

I took it because I had to. Sure, I still love dancing, and even the stripping side of it is enjoyable, but it's the job. The drunk, creepy men. The late, sleepless nights. The coming home stinking of alcohol and sweat.

If only I could be some sort of personal stripper—a live in stripper. Wow, wouldn't that be perfect?

"Where've you gone?" Clint murmurs, pushing a strand of hair behind my ear as we ride up in the elevator.

I didn't even realise we'd started to move.

"Sorry," I breathe, clearing my head of tragic thoughts. "Were you saying something?"

He simply smiles and shakes his head.

The doors open and I'm greeted by Ezra, whose hands are in his jogger pockets that fit so well on his muscled body.

"Oh," I squeak as he strides forward and wraps his arms around me in a hug. I don't miss a beat before returning the gesture. "Are you okay?"

He pulls back and nods. "Come." That's all he says—the word sounding dirty as fuck coming off of his tongue—before he wraps his hand around mine and drags me towards the hallway.

I chuckle nervously as Clint follows close

behind, his laugh almost rumbling like he's entertained. "Ezra?" I question, before I'm pulled through to my— To the spare bedroom.

Immediately, my eyes go wide and my breathing halts.

Woah is all I can think.

The walls—once a barren white—are now painted a light sapphire. A bright pink rug sits at the bottom of the bed, matching the bed sheets with intricate patterns. Plants and trinkets that I immediately fall in love with are littered around the open spaces, filling it almost completely so it looks bare no longer. A bookshelf now sits across the once empty wall, filled with…

"Oh my..!" I gasp, my fingers trailing across the books that are all, very clearly, dirty daddy romances.

I should be embarrassed or ashamed, but really, I'm fucking excited.

It's then I notice my teddy—that was once nestled into the pillows of the bed—is sitting neatly on the plush chair in the corner.

140

I dart forward and snatch it up, hiding it behind my back as I stand before the two of them.
It's an intimate and embarrassing part of myself.
To cling to this gross looking teddy that probably
wasn't even from anyone meaningful.

"Oh, sweet girl," Clint coos, and I imagine
his hand running over my hair. "Are you embarrassed about your teddy?" I don't move as he
steps forward to meet me, holding a hand out to
trail it down my cheek.

When I don't answer, he moves his palm to
grasp my jaw. "I asked you a question." His
voice is stern and sends goosebumps down my
spine.

I swallow, but nod, finally realising I feel
comfortable somewhere for the first time in my
life. Ezra moves to stand beside his friend and
wraps a strand of my freshly done hair around his
finger.

"Why are you embarrassed, doll?" Ezra asks
in a low tone, tugging ever-so-slightly on the
thick strand.

"It's silly," I whisper. He clicks his tongue like he's disappointed in me. Immediately, I bristle.

"No, it's not." He shakes his head softly. "Tell us."

I exhale but bring Mr Jeffers out from behind me to rest against my stomach protectively. "This is Mr Jeffers." They both raise their brows and lower their gazes. "He…comforts me."

"How *old* is that thing?" Ezra says suddenly. Clint scowls and shoves his elbow into his friend's side. Ezra jerks up, clearly about to spit some venom, before catching sight of my wounded gaze. "Shit, doll, I'm sor—"

As he reaches his hand out to my face, I step back, shaking my head. Why would he insult my teddy? It's the one goddamn thing I have and he's *making fun* of it. Of *me*.

I hug Mr Jeffers to my chest, but as I turn away to hide the unshed tears, pressure wraps around my arm to tug me back gently. "Look at me," Ezra murmurs, his voice low and demanding.

I ignore him, breathing heavy as I stare off out the massive window that splays over the city.

He grasps my chin and pulls me to look at him. I jerk my gaze down to the floor where our feet almost touch. "Look. At. *Me*."

I want to ignore him, to continue nibbling on my bottom lip as I try to pretend he hasn't just blatantly humiliated me, but I don't.

Slowly, worried I'll find him filled with amusement, I lift my eyes to connect with his, where I see anything but.

"Oh, doll, I didn't mean to upset you." His soft tone wrenches at my heart and when he moves his hand to brush through my hair, a tear slips free.

Fuck, why am I so damn emotional? Why is everything they're saying getting to me?

Daddy issues, daddy issues, daddy issues!

"Shh, shh," he coos, using his thumb to swipe away the tears. "Don't cry, baby."

I don't know if it's the humiliation or the

compassion that makes me feel safer than I've ever felt before which makes me buckle, but I do, *hard*.

A sob breaks free from my throat as tears spill down my face and I shove myself against him, gripping at his shirt as I bawl into it. All the emotion, confusion and overwhelmingness of the past few days crashes into me like a tsunami. He immediately wraps his arms around me tight, nuzzling his face into my hair.

"Baby doll, please don't cry. I'm sorry. I'm so, so sorry. I didn't mean to upset you. I'm jealous, that's all."

His words break through the pounding in my head from crying, and the tears slow as I pull back. "What?" I rasp, not lessening my grip on him. "Jealous of what?"

He sighs, eyeing the teddy I'm still grasping between my fingers. "Who got you the bear, Aida?"

My brows are furrowed as I answer, "My dad, apparently."

"Apparently?" he questions, and I nod.

"That's what I was told, but he isn't a good man… I think it was the hospital or some random nurse," I shrug, my heart hurting all over again.

Ezra's grip on my arm becomes tight momentarily before it's released. "He doesn't deserve you. He doesn't deserve to be the one to give you this. I'm jealous because… I want to be the one to give you teddies."

I blink at him, and then Clint, who's standing behind him with his arms folded, watching the situation unfold with blatant amusement.

"I want to be your *daddy*."

EIGHT

 **EZRA**

A few days ago, I stubbed my toe on the corner of the island in the kitchen space. In that moment, and ever since, I've believed that was the worst pain I have ever—or will ever—feel.

But watching my sweet doll cry and feeling her wet tears against my shirt beats it by miles.

She sniffles up at me as she processes what I say. That's right, baby. I want to be your daddy.

"W-what?" she sputters, eyes darting back and forth between Clint and I.

"I—" I'm cut off as Clint clears his throat from behind me, and I roll my eyes. "*We* want to be what you need, Aida. We want to be—"

"My daddies," she breathes, eyes wide with wonder. My cock reacts to her breathy tone and the words she accompanies with it. "You want to be my daddies?"

I nod and watch as Clint moves to stand behind her so she's sandwiched between us. "We want to take care of you," he whispers, trailing his nose up her neck. "We want to make sure you feel special and wanted." And loved.

There's silence as she no doubt processes what we're saying to her. "You…*do*?"

"Of course we do," I sigh, absently running my fingers up the side of her waist. "It's all we think about."

"Have you—" She clears her throat, twisting in my hold so her sides are pressed against both of our chests, allowing her to flick those beautiful, pastel green eyes between us. "Have you done this before?"

"Never," we immediately say in sync, wanting her to know just how deep our adoration runs for her.

I continue, feeling slightly nervous as I begin to lay myself out for her, something I've never done before for anyone apart from Clint.

"I know I'm not as conversational or smooth as Clint, but I've never exactly wanted to be for anyone before you, little doll. But I need you, and everything you have to offer."

She swallows and wearily eyes Clint, waiting for him to say his piece. He doesn't miss a beat and kisses her cheek, pulling back with a twist of her hair—that's now a brighter pink than the faded, almost muted colour it was before—around his finger.

"There's a lot about us you don't know yet, sweet girl, but we want you to know it all. We want you to let us care for you like you deserve, to lie back and let us look after you like you always should have been."

I see the uncertainty in her eyes. I think

about how much I can't wait until she truly understands how we feel about her.

Would we ever tell her about how we watched her—*stalked* her—from afar? Would she run for the hills?

"Is it crazy that I want that?" she whispers, twisting her hands around the tatted bear nervously. I restrain an angry, almost primal remark from my throat at the sight, but as badly as I want to destroy the thing, I know it brings her peace and serenity, so for that, I'll allow it.

But I *will* be attempting to wean her off onto ones from Clint and I—without a doubt.

"Not at all," my best—only—friend whispers into her ear. "But if it does, then Ezzie and I are undoubtedly insane."

She lets out a sweet giggle that has me blowing out a sigh of relief as she looks up at me. "Ezzie, huh?"

I roll my eyes but can't help grinning, swiping my lips across her forehead without actually putting pressure down. "Wanna play games, little girl? I've got games."

The corner of her lips tilt up in what looks like a challenge and I want to punish the fuck out of her until she's a writhing, over-stimulated mass of slumped bones between Clint and I.

"How do you like your room?" I ask instead, adoring the way her eyes look less worried and more excited.

"*My* room?" she squeaks, eyes widening to an almost comical size.

"It's been yours since we met you," Clint smiles, his words not being a total lie but not admitting the whole truth. "Ezra was looking forward to decorating it for you."

She's startled, clearly, as she does another spin, taking in the room. I love the way her eyes linger on the bookshelf filled with dirty and—apparently, according to the librarian who recommended them to Clint—sweet books about age-gap romances.

"It's amazing, but—"

"If you say *too much*, I'm bending you over

my knee and leaving my handprint on your ass," Clint spits, pushing himself into her backside, effectively squeezing her beautiful body against mine.

She gasps, and no doubt she can feel how hard my cock is against her stomach.

"But I bet you'd like that, wouldn't you?" I whisper, revelling in her shivers as I run my fingertips over her skin. "I bet you'd adore resting over our knees, you're ass in the air, ready to take what we give you."

"You'd take it all, wouldn't you, sweet girl?" Clint brushes her hair over her shoulder. "Everything we give you."

She whimpers, letting her head roll back onto his shoulder as she rubs her thighs together. I almost combust at the thought of the soft skin slick with her need, readying her to take both of us.

Which she *will*.

But just as I'm about to press my thigh to her mound and order her to grind herself to release, her stomach grumbles, *loud*.

"Poor girl," Clint sighs, pressing a kiss to her ear. "Food, or orgasm?"

"Food," I grind out immediately. "She's going to sit there and eat her food like a good girl whilst her pussy drips onto our seats."

She bites her lip and scrunches her eyes shut, no doubt imagining filthy, *filthy* things.

"Won't you be a good girl and join us for dinner again, doll?"

She pries her eyes open to look at me, all needy and filled with lust. She nods, like she can't speak, but I brush her curls away anyway and say, "Good girl."

A blush that's crept up her chest, neck and cheeks intensifies, and she twitches on the spot as she rubs her thighs once again.

Oh, my girl definitely has a thing for praise, but I'll take my time *confirming* this.

I swallow a chuckle at the thought.

Both her and Clint follow me to the dining area, Aida between us as my best friend no doubt watches the curve of her ass when she walks.

I pull out her chair for her, tuck her back in and press a kiss to the top of her head.

I've been preparing a meal since lunch time and begin to serve it up, making a point to give Clint and I cutlery but not Aida.

I sit down next to her and watch as her eyebrows furrow in confusion. "Oh, erm—"

I lift my food-covered fork to her lips. She looks even more confused for a moment before I push it further and her eyes widen in realisation.

"Open up, pretty girl." She does so, *slowly*, her lips glistening like an offering. I slip the fork in and watch just as intently as Clint does as she takes it and chews. When she swallows, I take some more. "Good girl."

A noise that sounds like a broken whimper comes from her throat. Oh yeah, *definitely* a lover of praise. How perfect is she?

As I continue to feed her, I can tell she's beginning to enjoy it. "Tell us, Aida," Clint starts, wrapping her hand in his from where he sits across from us. "Do you need to be taken care of?"

I see immediately when her hackles rise as she pulls away from both of us, shaking her head. "No," she says adamantly.

"Liar," he whispers softly, his gaze turning to one of patronising pity and I'm excited to see this unfold. "Are you lying to me, Aida?"

She's conflicted. She wants to give in, to play our little game and let loose. To allow someone to take care of her.

But the other side of her—the side that fears being isolated and broken again, the side that has taken care of her for years—is fighting against it.

Clint pushes without an answer. "Do you know what happens to lying little girls, hmm?" Her breath hitches. I see her resolve begin to dissipate. "They get punished."

Her lips part, her eyes go wide with expectation.

I take that chance to push another forkful into her mouth, needing to take care of her before anything happens.

Her eyes move from Clint's to mine as I continue to feed her, never breaking the connection. Tension floods the room, the silence louder than any sound.

I pick up the glass of fresh water and push it to her lips. A few drops slip down her chin and when I pull away, the sight of it—along with the liquid coating her plump lips—makes my dick pulse behind my trousers.

I'm not sure why I open my mouth to ask this, but I do. "How come you haven't got a boyfriend, doll?"

She snaps her eyes up and narrows them, thinking about my question. "Because they never stay."

Her words sound broken and filled with emotion, wrenching my heart. No, I don't want any other man—apart from Clint—touching her, caring for her, *loving* her, but the thought of my lovely Aida feeling anything but positive emotions makes me want to rub at my aching chest.

I nod, pushing away my own emotions to focus on hers, indicating she should continue. She flicks her gaze between Clint's and mine with uncertainty, most likely wondering why the sudden change, but my business partner is just as curious as I am.

"They said I was…high maintenance. That I was too much effort for someone who…*whored around*."

"And are you?" I ask, tilting my head. "High maintenance?"

Her sad, soft gaze turns sharp, giving me a glimpse of my snarky, hardened girl. "No," she spits, no doubt feeling defensive.

Silly girl, when will she learn that I want *all* of her, every single little high maintenance piece and more?

"Are you *sure*?" Clint drawls, his elbows leaning on the table as he watches her intently. "Do you need caring for, Aida? To be looked after and protected? There's nothing wrong with it, sweet girl. Ezra and I simply want to know what makes you *happy*."

My fiery girl knows when to quit and her shoulders slump slightly as her fight turns into something else. Her head tilts forward like she's embarrassed and trying to subtly shrink into herself.

"I don't *like* being this way," she admits, tugging on my heart strings in a way I haven't felt many times since I left my past behind and focused on my career. "I've never felt protected, or *safe*."

"Did your father never make you feel safe?" I question. She's shocked at my blunt words, but she doesn't lie. In fact, she doesn't answer at all, but that says so much more than she possibly could.

I click my tongue and reach out to stroke the back of my knuckles down her cheek. "Baby," I sigh. "You *deserve* to feel safe and protected. Let us give that to you. At least for the next three days."

I expect to wait, but immediately she smiles

and nods. "I promised you three more days, you have those to do as you wish."

Oh, baby doll, you have *no* idea what you're getting yourself into with that promise.

"How does a bath feel, sweet?" Clint asks with a smile as he stands and walks around to be beside her. She sighs and straightens, taking his extended hand.

"That sounds nice." Her voice is much more relaxed than it has been and I feel relief at seeing her settling.

I jump up to follow because I'll be damned if Clint gets *more* time alone. Oh yeah, I'm no idiot, I *know* something went down between those two whilst they were out. But I'll wait for Clint to tell me, or maybe Aida, and then I'll fuck my fist to the thought.

She follows him through to the main, shared bathroom, and as soon as I shut the door, he's lifting her. She squeals in surprise as he plants her on the countertop beside the sink.

"Stay," he orders, before turning to start her

bath. She laughs and swings her legs with a soft smile, looking completely relaxed in our home.

I take this chance to sidle up beside her and lean against the counter. She turns to face me, her smile widening. I can't help myself, I have to trace the tip of her mouth with my finger.

She turns her head to press her lips fully against my skin, planting a kiss on my second and third finger.

And now I'm done.

I wrap my arm around her waist and pull her forward to meet my lips in a rush. She lets out a noise of surprise that quickly turns into a groan as she fists my shirt.

Her lips are soft and fucking perfect against mine. Everything feels like it fits into place now I have her in my arms, safe in my home.

I've been waiting two years for this woman, this unbelievably strong and brave woman who stole my heart in a matter of seconds. Now that I have her, I can hardly think straight.

I groan against the feel of her, the sound of

water running filling the room.

She moves against me without restraint, clinging to my shirt that needs to be removed in the next five seconds.

One hand goes to the back of her head where I fist her hair from the roots, holding her against me. She pulls my bottom lip between her teeth and bites down, smirking as she pulls away.

"I'll punish you later," I mumble, pressing kisses over her cheek and down to her jaw. She laughs lightly before moaning when my teeth nip at her neck.

The water stops, but I don't want to let her go. I never want to let her go.

She threads her hands through my hair. My kisses against her skin become frantic, lust taking over every sense.

"Aida," I sigh, running my fingers under the hem of her favourite hoodie. Her legs wrap around me and I use my grip on her waist to lift her up and slip the material over her head.

She jumps against the temperature of the

counter when I place her back down, but all I can think about is how she looks in her little red lacy bra and panties.

I'm done for.

She uses her hold on my waist and digs her block-heeled boots into my ass, dragging me forward. The fabric of my trousers does nothing to hide the warmth of her pussy beneath the thin scraps of material as she presses against my cock.

We groan in unison. I can't help the small thrust of my hips. She leans her head back to moan, wrapping her arms around my neck to pull me as close as possible.

"Fuck, doll." She tilts her head as I leave more kisses up her skin, my cock throbbing as she uses her hold to pull me back and forth against her.

"Ezra," she whimpers, the sound better than music to my fucking ears. "Oh, *fuck.*"

I need more.

I slip my fingers into her panties, giving her

the time to stop this if she isn't ready.

But instead, my girl only nods erratically, staring at where I'm now touching. She bucks against me as I connect my fingers to her soaking pussy, pressing down on her clit.

She whimpers, the sound almost enough to have me grinding against her leg for some type of relief.

"Ezra!" she gasps. "Oh fuck, oh fuck. Yes, right there, don't stop."

There isn't much that could make me.

With a thumb to her clit, I slip two fingers inside of her. She arches her back and cries out, gripping onto me like I might leave if she lets go. Never, doll.

"Clint's waiting to bathe you," I whisper, keeping my rhythm to the same fast pace. "Come for us, doll. Come all over my fingers, soak them, squeeze them."

Her lips part on a silent scream as she follows my demand, the tight hole of her cunt squeezing me so beautifully I picture how good it'll feel when it's my cock.

Our sweet doll is so sensitive and responsive, her whole body shaking with aftershocks as I slow my pace down to draw her orgasm out.

I skim her clit—not accidentally, but she doesn't know that—and chuckle as her entire body jerks. Fuck, she's so sensitive to touch. I can't wait until we're reducing her to nothing but a writhing mess.

Her breathing is laboured as she comes down from her high, not loosening her grip on my shoulders until Clint comes to stand by my side.

"Beautiful," he murmurs, pressing a rough kiss to her swollen lips.

I take my two fingers to stick them in my mouth, adoring the way she tastes. I can't fucking wait to eat her pussy. "Delicious, too."

Clint almost growls and wraps his hand around my wrist, pulling my hand to his face before I suck my fingers the whole way in.

He wraps his lips around them and sucks off

the rest of Aida's release. "Oh fuck," she breaths, staring at us wide-eyed. Clint and I aren't into each other like that, but we don't have normal boundaries, and she seems to be enjoying it.

Clint crouches down to his knees—something that has *never* happened before—and gently lifts Aida's leg to unzip her shoe. He slips it off with care before doing the same to the other.

"Come," Clint demands, lifting her up as she goes floppy in his arms and allows him to transport her to the bath.

He lowers her into the water and we both revel in her beautiful sigh. We know she didn't own a bath in her old, tiny house that was ran by a sexist pervert, so we're glad to offer her this small relief.

"Is that okay?" he asks softly, sitting on the edge of the tub. She nods, her eyes closed and a blissful smile playing on her lips.

I don't want to disturb her peace, so I leave without a word.

I put away her shopping, hanging it up or

folding it into her drawers, and pull out a set of pyjamas we bought when preparing for her.

They're made of white silk with a cherry pattern printed over it.

I head back into her bathroom, just as Clint's helping her out with a towel waiting in his open arms. "All done?" I ask, pulling out her hairbrush and laying it on the counter.

She beams up at me with a beautiful smile that forces my heart into nothing but a puddle. Clearing my throat, I offer her the tank top and shorts set.

She dries off quickly whilst I force myself to respectfully avert my eyes and switches her towel with the pyjamas before slipping them on. She looks adorable.

"Turn," I say, not giving her much of an option as I spin her so her back is facing me.

Using the brush, I begin to work through her hair. She sighs and lets her head drop.

The thick, pink strands feel smooth beneath my skin, and I can't help adoring the way they

165

move across my fingers.

We've taken a massive step forward, and a weight I didn't even know I've been harbouring on my chest feels as though it's been lifted into the air, pried away by her fingers.

I think we have a chance.

NINE

It's been two days since they found me and swept me off my feet. As I lie here in the soft, purple bed sheets with sweet-smelling skin and freshly brushed hair, I run that thought through my mind.

Two down, three to go.

It's not normal to want someone *this* much in such a short space of time, is it? Because that's the truth. I really, *really* want them, so much so that I've found myself throwing caution to the wind and trusting them both with my body.

Because, somehow, I actually *do* trust these two men.

Now, I lay here on my back, propped up by fluffy pillows, staring out at the city lights from the comfort of this dim room. They even provided me with a little night light on the bedside table I can control, but I feel lonely now they left me with parting kisses to the cheek and sweet goodnights.

It's not *enough*.

I slip out of the sheets, my bare feet finding the pink rug atop the wooden floorboards. I pad along them, opening the door slightly to peer out into the dark hallway.

It creaks slightly as I pull it back further to allow access for my body to slip through. It's silent, and almost eerie with how cold the rest of the penthouse is compared to my homey room. Why have they never settled into this place?

I feel like a child sneaking around, doing something I shouldn't. Except, I'm a grown woman, so why does this still feel so fun?

My palm wraps around the handle leading into Clint's room—I'm still getting a grasp on both of them, but I feel as though he's the one most likely to let me snuggle up with him—and twist, my heart slightly racing for some reason.

Why am I nervous? Is it the darkness surrounding me as I creep through these halls? Is it the anticipation of sneaking into his room, unknowing?

I push forward, cringing at the creak from both the floorboard and door. The room is dark, not pitch-black but close, as I poke my head in and blink, attempting to adjust to the light.

I scan the room, noticing the dark curve in the bed beneath the sheets. I slip through and shut the door behind me as quietly as possible before taking a couple of steps towards the bed.

As I stand at the side of his bed and peer over him, feeling like a major creep, I watch his brows furrow momentarily and his lips inch downwards in a sleepy frown.

He twitches, and a moment later, he's

blinking awake. "Aida?" he asks groggily, slowly sitting himself up. "Baby, are you okay?"

"Lonely," I whisper, wrapping my arms around myself, feeling slightly stupid now. "I don't want to sleep alone, Clint."

He wakes up almost instantly, eyes wide, quickly shuffling to the middle of the bed and pulling the sheets back.

"Shit, I'm sorry, sweet girl," he murmurs as I join him, nestling in close as he tucks me into his side. I immediately feel safer. "I thought you'd want your space, is all. I didn't mean to upset you."

He presses a soft kiss to the top of my head. "Do you need anything?"

I sigh in content and shake my head against his chest. "Just hold me tight," I murmur, my eyes hurting from exhaustion.

They flutter shut, and I fall asleep with his promise of, "Always."

"SHE LOOKS SO BEAUTIFUL."

I keep my body lax against the heat wrapped around me, my eyes still shut as sleep fades away. The first thing I notice is the soreness in my throat, understanding immediately the first sign of the common cold.

It wasn't Clint who spoke, but I feel his chest rumble as he hums his agreement.

"So beautiful," he coos, pressing a kiss to the top of my head. He's still holding me tight to his body, my head nestled atop his naked chest. "Are you jealous?" He doesn't say this teasingly, but like he's actually curious.

I don't want to alert them that I'm awake, so I keep my breathing steady.

"Kind of," Ezra—the second person in the room, *obviously*—sighs, and there's pressure on the bed beside me as he no doubt sits down next to me. "I'm happy she trusts you enough, I just…"

"Want it to be you?" Clint finishes for him. There's no reply, but I imagine Ezra nodding his head. The back of a finger trails over my cheek in a soft line. "It'll come."

"I hope so." My heart wrenches at the sad tone of his voice. Does he not think I trust him? Does he think I somehow *prefer* Clint?

"Ezzie?" I murmur, turning in Clint's hold to face him, my eyes opening slowly. His eyes are already on me, but his eyebrows rise slightly.

"Sorry." He immediately stands to back away, guilt etched over his face, but I dart forward and grip his hand.

"Stay," I order, gently pulling him back down to his sitting position.

"I'm sorry," he repeats. "I only wanted to check on you. I was worried. I didn't mean—"

"Stop." He does so, his eyes not leaving mine. "I'm not ready to get up. Do you have anywhere you need to be?"

He's not dressed as though he does, in a loose white t-shirt and a pair of joggers. "No."

I pat the space beside me. "Lie with me, Ezzie."

He swallows, flicks a glance at his best friend, before twisting to lie against the headboard, keeping a small, yet respectful, distance.

I don't like that, so I swing my leg and arm over his body, nuzzling into his side. Clint follows, keeping close so I'm pressed between both of them.

"I trust you both," I admit in a whisper. "It doesn't always seem like you're up to talk, or hang. I thought Clint might be more open to cuddling."

Ezra makes a sound of disapproval, his arm slipping around my waist to rest beside Clints. "I always want to talk to you, Aida. I always want to be around you. I'll *always* want to cuddle."

I smile, but it drops when I swallow, hating how it feels like ingesting a cheese grater. "Are you okay?" Clint whispers, his fingers moving in circles on my skin.

"I think I'm coming down with something." A cough bubbles up in my chest that hurts when I let it out. My nose is also starting to run, but so far, it just seems like a very, very mild cold. "I'll be okay."

"Let me get you some tea," Clint offers, but before I can assure him I'm fine, he unwraps himself and darts out the room.

"Do you need anything else?" Ezra asks, pulling me tighter against him so my head is nuzzled beneath his. I have never felt as safe as I do here, lying in Clint's bed with a protective arm wrapped around me from Ezra.

I shake my head because I know he can feel me against him. "Really, I'm fine. I get colds like this all the time. It'll pass quickly."

"Doesn't mean we like the thought of you being in pain, no matter how small," he admits. I sigh—a happy noise—and snuggle in tighter as though I'm trying to bury myself under his skin.

I have never, once in my life, felt like this. I've had boyfriends, but in years they couldn't make me feel what these men have made me feel in mere days.

His fingers run smooth circles over the open

skin on my waist, eliciting a different type of feeling. I shiver, wrapping my leg tighter around his hips. My senses suddenly feel heightened, and the press of something firm beneath my thigh makes me almost whimper with want.

"You feel that, doll?" he whispers, stroking soothing touches over my head. "That's what being around you does to me."

I pull my arm back from his waist and place my hand on his chest before slowly, *tauntingly*, dragging it down his body.

His toned stomach flexes under my touch, as if I affect him as much as he affects me, and he lets out a low, shaky breath, not letting up his tender strokes.

I reach the waistband of his joggers and slip my fingertips beneath.

"Aida, baby, you don't have to—"

I wrap my hand around his—woah, *large* cock, cutting him off with a low groan. "I want to," I whisper, because I really do. With other guys, they always made sex seem like a chore, but already these two have focused on *me* with rapt attention and admiration.

I'd suck his cock for hours, I'd let him cover me in his cum, and I'd *more* than enjoy it.

His strokes become a tight grip on my hair and his breaths become heavy as I slowly start to move my hand up and down. "Fuck, Aida."

I pull my head back to look up at him. He meets my eyes immediately. His gaze is filled with lust and I adore the way he places a hand to my cheek and crashes his lips onto mine.

I rub my thumb over his tip, smearing pre-cum around the head. His hips twitch at the feel. His hand slides from my cheek to grip the back of my hair.

"I want to let you set the pace, baby, but fuck I want to feel your mouth."

I don't want to set the pace. I want to let go completely, to be controlled and cared for, knowing I'm safe.

"Use me," I whisper, "Use me, and take care of me. I don't want to be in control of my body,

Ezra, *please*—"

He cuts me off with a tug at my hair before urging me down. I follow more than willingly, placing my hands on either of his thighs to steady myself.

I pull his joggers down, letting them rest beneath my legs, and use one hand to angle him up towards me. His grip on my hair feels perfect as he guides me down.

My lips part as I wrap them around the head of his fat cock.

"Tap my thigh twice if you need to come up," he orders, and before I can reply, he thrusts up roughly, immediately hitting the back of my throat.

I adore the feeling, how helpless I am to him knowing he'd never hurt me. At least, that's how I feel. This could be the stupidest choice I've ever made, trusting these two, but I don't allow those thoughts to take over.

I deserve this.

He doesn't stop, using his grip on my hair to

keep me in place as he fucks my mouth.

"That's it, that's it." He throws his head back and clenches his eyes shut. "Perfect, perfect girl."

His praise makes me whimper, sending heat straight to my cunt, but also wrapping me in a tight, safe embrace.

"Fuck, I'm not going to last long with a mouth like yours, doll." I double down my efforts, hollowing my cheeks, internally begging for his cum down my throat. "God, you want it so bad, don't you?"

I nod, the movement barely noticeable, but a moment later, his grip tightens on my hair almost painfully as he holds his cock in my mouth, groaning loudly whilst he fills my throat with cum.

As soon as he's emptied himself inside of me, and I eagerly swallow it, he tugs me up to sit atop him, straddling his waist. He puts two hands on either side of my face before pulling me down as he arches up so we meet in a sweet kiss.

"I meant it," I whisper, teasing my bottom lip over his. "I trust you and Clint the same. I don't have a favourite. I like you *both* very much."

His smile is lazy and sated, somehow boyish on his older features, and it's sexy as fuck.

"Fuck," someone mutters behind me. I turn my head to see Clint leaning on the door frame, a cup of tea in his hand and a very noticeable dent in his joggers. "Throat feeling better now, sweet?"

I scrunch my nose and stick my tongue out at him before turning and burying my face into Ezra's shoulder, feeling his body shake with quiet laughter.

I hear Clint move around the room, then the clang of glass atop ceramic as he places the mug on the bedside table. "Come on, doll," Ezra murmurs, sitting up and bringing me with him.

I pull back as he grabs the handle and puts the edge to my lips. His other hand is at the back of my head, controlling my movements as he

179

urges the liquid down my throat.

It feels good to both soothe the soreness of my throat and to quench my thirst. "Good girl," he coos, pulling back when he can tell I've had my fill.

Clint stands beside us and Ezra helps me twist on his lap so my legs hang over the edge and I'm facing his best friend. Clint reaches out and touches two fingers underneath my chin, pressing slightly to bring my gaze to his.

"Did Ezra's cum help your tight little throat, sweet girl?" My cheeks flush red and hot, my head bowing slightly so my pink curls fall over my face.

Ezra doesn't miss a beat before he's pulling my hair back and wrapping it around his fist. He tugs, his grip firm as he holds me in place for Clint. My lips part open on their own accord and I feel like I'm being put on show for the both of them.

"Are you not going to answer?" he asks, staring down at me with his searing gaze. His fingers beneath my chin don't stop me from answering, but the bratty-ness inside me does.

I roll my eyes and fold my arms.

My determination falters ever so slightly when I see a smirk grow on his lips, like he's happy with my argument.

"Oh, *sweet girl*," he sighs, wrapping his hand around the back of my neck and tugging me up to stand before him, my hair slipping out of Ezra's hold. "Is that how you want to play this? Is your pretty cunt weeping after choking on Ezra's big cock, hm? You need to be taught some respect?"

Instead of shaking my head, turning submissive at his words, I raise my head and glare at him. He seems all too happy with this response.

He leans into my ear and whispers loud enough for both Ezra and I to hear. "Red for stop, yellow for pause, green for continue, alright?"

It takes me a second to understand, but when I do, my heart begins to race. I nod instantly and he pulls back with a smirk.

Then, before I can comprehend, he spins me around and bends me at the waist, my hands coming to land on Ezra's thighs where he sits on the edge of the bed.

My pink curls fall forward. He swipes them back and wriggles his fingers in greeting. My ass is on view for Clint, the small satin shorts not doing much to keep me hidden.

"Such a filthy little girl, isn't she, Ezzie?" The man in question nods immediately, rubbing a thumb over my cheek. "Your ass is perfect, sweet girl, but I want to paint it red."

He grips the waistband of my shorts before tugging, the material falling to the floor around my feet. Both of the men suck in a breath, and when I look up, Ezra's eyeing the view over my shoulder.

"No panties, little girl?" Clint says angrily, leaning over me to cover my body with his and put his mouth to my ear. "That's an extra five. You're going to count, and you're going to enjoy. Got it?"

He pulls back. I'm about to ask what's happening when he brings his palm down on my ass, a loud smack reverberating through the room.

My ass stings, and I cry out, but Clint's immediately rubbing the sore skin.

"Colour?"

It takes me a moment to catch my breath, but I adore the way Ezra is looking down at me as if I'm absolute perfection. "Green," I pant, squirming between them. "One."

"Good girl," Ezra praises, just as Clint spanks my other cheek. "Our sweet, perfect girl."

"Two," I groan, falling forward slightly to bury my face in Ezra's lap.

He brings it down again. A moan is ripped from my throat. "Three."

"Look at how well she's taking it," Ezra sighs, playing with my hair.

"She's fucking adoring it," Clint replies, before his hand begins to slip lower until he's pressing against my inner thigh. "I'm not even touching her cunt and I can feel her skin slick with need."

"Is that right?"

I rub my thighs together, trying my hardest to push him closer to where I really need him. "Greedy girl," he mutters before lightly slapping my clit.

I cry out, my fingers curling into the material of Ezra's joggers. I feel tears pool against my bottom lashes but I clamp them shut as Clint spanks me another time.

These men have taken my heart and shoved themselves deep inside. This endless feel of safety wrenches at my chest but I can't find it in myself to care anymore. Doubt? I've chucked it out the window. Letting them take care of my body—or *punish* it—so well, allowing me to just feel, is blissful.

When I don't count, Ezra tips my face up to meet him. "Open your eyes, doll." I do, but when I'm met with the sweetest look of adoration from this man, more tears spill. "Shh, shh." He slips his hands under my arms, but as soon as I realise he's going to pick me up, I bat at him.

"Four," I rasp, pushing back so my ass meets Clint's covered cock. "More. *More*."

"Colour?" Clint whispers, stroking down my back.

"Green. So fucking green." The burn on my skin feels beautiful, but I want his print on me more than anything. I realise I've worried them, which I have to change. "Spank me before I finish myself off in the bathroom, daddy."

Ezra shakes his head with a silent chuckle as Clint whispers, "Fuck," and a moment later, he's gifting me number five.

He doesn't stop there. Ezra continues to soothe me as Clint spanks me until we're at number ten, and by then, I'm a pent up, whimpering mess.

This time, when Ezra slips his hands under my arms and drags me up to straddle his lap, I don't protest. His smile brightens my own.

"What happened, sweetness?" Clint asks from behind as he places his hands on my waist.

Ezra begins kissing down my neck, and I'm so turned on that the light touches feel anything but light.

"I've never felt like this with anyone before," I finally admit, my hands curling into the material of Ezra's shirt. "You make me feel safe."

TEN

Clint

I don't think I've ever been this on the verge of coming in my pants.

We make her feel *safe*. She *wants* us.

That's not good enough. She has to need us as much as we need her—but we'll get there.

"Our perfect girl," Ezra whispers after he's regained himself. I still haven't.

He grips the back of her head and brings her forward, smashing his lips against hers in a kiss filled with need and passion. She whimpers against him as he tugs her bottom lip between his teeth.

"You took me so well," I finally say, grasping her jaw and turning her to face me. "I'm so proud of you, sweet girl."

I take her in for my own kiss, capturing her soft, beautiful lips with urgency—because that's what I always am: urgent for her.

I pull away and push her down by a hand on her back, Ezra lowering himself until he's lying down and she's flush against him.

"So beautiful," I murmur, pushing her little satin top up so I can explore the skin on her back with light, teasing touches.

"So perfect," Ezra sighs, pressing light kisses over her face.

I trail my fingers over her ass until I reach her glistening pussy on show for me now she's bent at the waist. It's a beautiful sight.

"Poor girl," I taunt, skimming my fingers up and down her inner thighs, so close to where she wants me but not close enough. "She's soaked, Ezra. So fucking soaked."

She makes a needy noise and attempts to

wriggle but Ezra's hold on her hips forces her still.

"Let me taste," he orders. I waste no time teasing her hole. She cries out and tries to move but I'm already pulling back.

I lean over the two of them and place my fingers at his lips. He eagerly takes me into his mouth, his eyes shutting as he moans around my fingers.

She stares at us with wide eyes. "Aw, does someone need release?" I tease, pulling my fingers out of Ezra's mouth just to slip them into hers. "I bet your tight little hole is twitching around nothing, hmm? Begging for our cocks?"

She nods erratically as she shifts her body forward and then back, grinding herself needily on Ezra's lap. He throws his head back against the bed.

"Fill her up before I do," he groans, clamping his eyes shut. "I'm not sure how much longer I'll last with her grinding on me."

I chuckle, though I don't even know how

long I'll last when I'm buried inside her. But for Aida? I'd last forever.

I slip my hand inside my joggers, my cock twitching in my palm as I rub precum around my tip. I don't want to wait but watching her pleasure herself on Ezra's lap is almost perfect.

And then it's not enough.

I strip off my joggers and grab myself at the base, stepping forward to put myself right in front of her slit. I push forward slightly, teasing my tip over her hole, relishing the way she moans and attempts to push herself back.

"You ready, sweetness?"

I don't let her answer before thrusting forward and filling her to the hilt.

She buries her head in Ezra's chest to muffle herself.

I groan at how good she feels. It's better than anything I've ever felt before.

I'm never letting her go.

I pull out and shove deep inside her again. Over and over, I fuck her as hard as physically possible, desperate to be as close to her as physically possible.

Ezra just watches her with a heated look in his eyes, but also admiration and obsession. It's the exact same way I feel.

"Aida, you feel so fucking good."

I can feel her getting close already, but one orgasm isn't enough. Not for my perfect girl. No, she deserves so much more.

"That's it, sweet girl. Come all over my cock, let me feel how tight you can squeeze me."

"Clint," she whines, her body a ball of need.

She cries out and the feel of her squeezing my cock almost drags me over the edge. She shivers and twitches beneath me as I slow my thrusts to drag her orgasm out, her sensitive little cunt spasming around my cock.

Eventually, she sighs, falling forward with a satiated smile. "Oh no," I laugh, gripping either one of her arms. I drag her back so my chest is flush against her. She looks like a glorious, spent offering for my best friend.

He doesn't even bother slipping out his joggers, pulling out his impressive cock and angling it upwards.

He sits up on his knees, tracing the tip over her clit. She twitches against him.

"Stop teasing me," she seethes. I chuckle and lay her down softly against Ezra, stepping back.

He smirks at me before lifting her and turning her around. He places her in the middle of the bed, forcing her on her knees and pushing her head into the sheets so she's on perfect view for him.

"Say that again," he orders, massaging her red cheeks. When she doesn't reply, he spanks her, *hard*. Harder than I'd done it—I'd wanted to test her before pushing her—but she fists the sheets and groans. "Say. That. *Again*."

She shakes her head against the bed, pushing her body back on her knees until her ass meets his cock. He leans over her and grinds himself into her.

My cock is leaking at the sight.

"That's what I thought," he spits, driving into her fully with one thrust. He pulls back and grips her hips, using them as he fucks her with abandon. "You were made for us, doll. You understand?"

The noises she makes are pure perfection as she takes everything he gives her.

"We're never letting you fucking go."

We're not. We're really not.

"You're ours to care for, to protect. You understand that, little doll?"

When she doesn't reply—probably because her beautiful face is squished into the sheets and the only noise she can make is a throaty whimper—he wraps an arm around her waist and tugs her up so her back is pressed against his front.

"I asked you a question," he grunts, punctuating each word with a thrust. "Do you understand?"

"Yes, yes," she cries, her voice hoarse.

"Yes what?" I ask, kneeling on the bed in

front of them, fisting my cock slowly.

"Yes, daddy," she manages to rasp out, and so I reward her. I stick two fingers in her mouth before pressing them to her swollen clit.

I rub in circles, and less than ten seconds later, she's screaming out her orgasm, her eyes rolling to the back of her head as she writhes against us.

Ezra's scrunching his eyes, no doubt trying to hold back his orgasm. I felt the struggle of keeping it together when such a perfect cunt squeezes you so tight.

She falls forward, right into my arms, but as I stroke her messy hair, I chuckle against her. "You think this is it, baby?" I ask.

She pulls back slightly, blinking. "What?"

Ezra swipes her hair back over her shoulder. She's a mess of sweat and blush, it's absolutely breathtaking. "We're not done with you, doll. Not by a long shot."

"But first." I kiss her softly on the lips before quickly retreating to the kitchen, where I fill a glass full of cold water. I rush back, desperate to see my girl already.

When I walk back through the room, both of them are completely naked, her breasts now on show. He's sitting up against the headboard and she's in his lap with his hands firmly grasping her ass as they kiss passionately.

I wrap her hair around my fist and pull back, her lips parting in invite. "Drink," I order, pressing the glass to her lips. Her eyes are wide and doe-like as she stares up at me, following my order. "Good girl," I murmur, using my grip on her head to gently massage her skin.

I can tell when she's had her fill and bring the now half-full glass to the bedside table. "Come here," Ezra sighs, pulling her back down to his lips.

"Tell me, sweetness." I move onto the bed behind her, skimming my hands over her shoulders and down her back. "Are you on birth control?"

I already know the answer, and a pang of

guilt shoots through my chest. Will we ever tell her the truth? That we've been watching her for two whole years? What if she leaves? I don't think either of us would survive—not emotion- ally.

"Yes," she breathes, and I push all negative thoughts aside. That can all come later, but right now, I need to be in this moment with both of them.

"Good." I press a kiss to her shoulder, her neck, and then her cheek. "Because we're going to fill you up with so much cum, you'll be over- flowing."

She inhales, but before she has a chance to respond, I grip her hip and fill her full of my cock, relishing in the sounds she makes and the feel of her little pussy.

I pull out slowly, staring with adoration as she swallows me whole. "Ezzie," she groans, her nails digging into his chest.

"I know, little doll. I know," he assures.

I fill her to the hilt and pause, pressing kiss

after kiss over her flushed neck.

I feel him shift beneath us, and a moment later, there's pressure against my cock. She sucks in a breath but doesn't relent.

"Quickly, or slowly?" He pushes in the tip ever so slightly, and I shiver at the feeling.

She doesn't answer immediately.

"Slowly, daddy. Stretch me out for you."

ELEVEN

I 've never felt so full, and he's only halfway in.

"You okay, sweetness?"

I nod, unable to form coherent sounds as Ezra continues to gently fill me up, stretching me wider than I've ever been before.

"You're doing so well, aren't you, doll? We're so proud of you."

I can't help but preen under his words, wanting to take them both to the hilt and feel their cum filling me, marking me.

"Almost there, baby, almost there." When they're both seated fully inside, they groan in unison, the sound spurring me on, making me clench around them.

"I'm not lasting long with a pussy like hers," Clint groans, resting his head on my shoulder.

"Me neither, so let's make her little cunt come before we fill her up."

And then they fuck me.

Their hands are everywhere, their words of pleasure and praise filling the room as they meld their bodies to mine.

They both feel unbelievably good, and I don't know how I'm ever going to live without them again. I don't want to.

"She's so fucking tight," Ezzie groans, thrusting into me from below, his grip on my skin punishing. "How did we go so long without her?"

"Never again," Clint says between clenched teeth. "Never, ever again. I'll die before I let her go."

They're talking about me like I'm not even there as they stare at me with lustful eyes, like it's not my choice whether I stay or go.

And at this point, I have no idea whether it is.

But I like it. I like the way they speak about me, the way they clearly care. I *crave* it.

"You like that, baby?" Clint murmurs, swiping my hair out my face as they both hammer into me with hard, rhythmic thrusts.

My body jerks with each pound, and my whimpers break into little noises as I nod my head, because I really do.

"You like that you've captured the both of us, *ensnared* us like a siren? Do you like how obsessed you've made us? Just watching you isn't enough, you're ours now."

I don't understand what he means by watching me, but my heart rate speeds up with some sort of excitement.

"She doesn't even realise what she's done to us," Clint scoffs, his hand going to wrap around my throat. "You've trapped us, sweetness. You've taken everything from our bodies with a smile. And we'll let you. We'll give it all freely, baby."

It's too much.

Their hands tightening around my hips and throat.

Their words filling the room, promising me everything I've ever dreamed of.

The feeling of them rutting into me like I'm nothing but a, well, *doll*.

But if I fall down this hole, will I ever get back? I'd be giving them everything, they could ruin me.

They could have done that by now. They don't need my acceptance and permission to ruin me. Why shouldn't I be given a break from this dreary world? Don't I deserve this?

Yes. Yes I do.

So, I give in.

"I'm yours," I gasp, my orgasm so close. "I want everything you have."

They both stop. They stop talking, stop moving, stop hammering into me.

I whine in protest, trying to move on both their cocks.

"Stop," Ezra orders, his voice low.

My heart feels like it's been pulled out of my chest at his tone, like I've said the wrong thing. Have they both just been talking in the heat of the moment? Sex and lust makes people say and do crazy things, but I thought this is real.

Suddenly, I feel stupid. More stupid than I've ever felt in my life.

Tears well up in my eyes, my cheeks heating and my ears burning from embarrassment. I reach over to run and remove myself from the situation, but Ezra tugs me back and presses me into Clint's chest.

Both of their cocks are still buried deep inside, and I feel them both twitch, but I daren't make a noise.

"You mean that, sweet girl?" Clint whispers, his chest heavy but comforting against my back.

"You're ours?"

I blink back the tears as I turn my head to try and look at him. "What?" I choke out, a tear managing to make its way down my cheek.

Ezra brings his hand up and uses his thumb to swipe away the tear. "Why are you crying, little doll?"

Clint immediately swats his hand away and grips my cheeks with one hand, squashing my mouth slightly as he tugs me to face him.

"Why are you crying?" he demands, his gaze narrow and frantic.

"Why are you angry at me?" I sob, muffled by my squished cheeks, feeling vulnerable and more than confused. I'm still naked, completely at their mercy with them inside of me, pressed between them.

Immediately, his face softens, his searing eyes turning compassionate. "Baby, we're not angry at you. I just want to know why you're crying. I hate seeing you cry."

I don't know how to *explain* why I'm upset.

"I-I thought I said the wrong thing, or some-thing," I mumble, letting my head tilt forward so my hair comes to shelter me like curtains. It's my usual reaction when feeling like I need to hide away.

They both tut, Ezra swiping my hair away from my face and gripping it at the base of my neck as Clint shakes his head. "No, baby, *no*. We're just…shocked. You said you want to be ours."

I flit my eyes between them, swallowing and nodding, taking a chance rather than denying it like I want to.

Both of their cocks twitch inside me again, and I moan, adoring the way they feel against each other.

"You don't understand what that means to us," Ezra sighs, pressing his forehead against mine.

"Can we please start fucking her now? I need to fill her with my cum, Clint. I need her to know she belongs to us."

My heart stutters at his words, all my fears immediately dissipating as Clint's lip tips up.

"You promise you're ours?" he whispers, and as soon as I nod, I realise I'm done for.

They move their hips in tandem, ruthlessly fucking me harder than before, like my words ignited something deep inside.

It doesn't take long before I tighten around their big cocks, coming so hard I shake and dig my nails into Clint's arms.

"Fuck yes," Clint shouts, gripping my hair and jackhammering into me. "I'm coming, I'm fucking coming."

Ezra's lips part as his eyes roll back, his stomach twitching as warm cum spurts inside of me. Their groans are deep and feral, the best sounds I've ever heard, and I know I'll do anything to hear them again.

My limbs go limp between them. They both breathlessly chuckle as Clint slips out and lies beside us, Ezra manoeuvring me so I'm comfortably sandwiched between them.

"Gods, I'm so fucking obsessed with you," Ezra mumbles into my neck, his arm coming to wrap around my waist.

I nuzzle into Clint's side, wrapping myself around him, adoring the way it feels to be completely surrounded by safety.

A part of me is relieved. They could have changed their minds as soon as they'd finished emptying themselves inside of me, as soon as the hazy lust barrier dissipated to leave us in reality, but they didn't. They've stuck to what they said and I can't be happier.

"How're you feeling now, sweetness?" Clint murmurs into the top of my head.

"Much better." It's the truth. Even if my throat still hurts and my muscles ache, it doesn't matter because my heart is finally full.

"GOOD GIRL," EZRA PRAISES, USING HIS

hold on my jaw to open my mouth and push in a spoonful of yoghurt. It's the only thing I want to eat today because of my throat.

It's been two days since they both took me at the same time and it's been nothing but pure bliss. They've taken care of me, nurtured me, spoiled me and obsessed over me non-stop, not once leaving the apartment.

Waking up this morning has been the worst, the cold I picked up hitting me full blast, but it just proves how much Ezra and Clint actually want me. My face is blotchy, my hair looks like a rat's nest, and I haven't spread my legs for them since the first time. Yet they haven't once looked at me with anything but pure adoration.

Ezra turned out to be the sweet, caring one. Don't get me wrong, they both are, but he *really* takes looking after me to the next level, which surprised me because he'd been so quiet and brooding when we first met.

But as I sit here, gulping down vanilla yoghurt, reality is seeping into my brain. I can't just live off these two, relying on them completely. I may trust them, and want them like I've never wanted anything before, but that doesn't mean I should turn docile and depend on them.

Which means finding my own place to stay, and getting back to work, which will happen tomorrow. I can tell the two of them have been dancing around the subject whenever I bring it up, but I don't have the energy to do that anymore.

"Ezra," I sigh before tightening my lips and shaking my head as he tries to give me more yoghurt.

"Open up, doll. You've not finished."

I wiggle my arm out from his grasp and cover my mouth so he can't slip it in when I'm talking—which he's done before. "No," I demand, my words slightly muffled. "No more."

He doesn't look happy, but obeys, and leaves the spoon in the pot of yoghurt. "Full, doll?"

I shake my head. "We need to talk. Where's

Clinton?"

He raises his eyebrows, most likely at the use of his best friend's full name. I like to use it when I'm being serious so they *know*-know.

His phone is laid out on the table, he quickly types a message before gripping my waist again. A moment later, Clint strides into the room.

"Everything okay, sweetness?" he asks, drying his hair with a towel as he quickly walks over.

"Sorry, I didn't mean to interrupt your shower."

He shakes his head. "Nonsense," he mutters, kissing the top of my head before leaning against the island, folding his arms to watch us. "You okay?"

I nod and try to squirm out of Ezra's lap, but he only wraps his arms around my waist and rests his chin on my head. "Ezra," I groan, shifting my shoulders in a half-assed attempt.

"Where are you going?" he questions.

I sigh, but give up, and let my body relax.

"I've got to get back to work tomorrow."

I feel his body go rigid against mine.

In the time I've spent here, they've not given me a single penny of their money—not that I want them to. They've bought absolutely everything I could possibly need or want and then some, but they've not given me any cash outright. So, I'm still just as bad off as before when it comes to a place to live, but now I've got fancy necklaces to wear as I cry on the street.

"I need to pick up more shifts so I can get a place to stay."

Ezra pulls back, his gaze searing into mine. "Stay with *us*," he growls, his fingers growing tight around my skin, almost punishing.

His words barely register in my head before Clint sits down beside us, moving me slightly so I'm resting on both of their laps.

"What he means is *please* stay with us," he sighs, playing with my hair. "We said we'd look after you, sweetness, and we meant it."

I flick my eyes between the two of them,

their words not exactly making sense. They want me to…what? *Live* with them?

"I-I can't just live with you," I scoff, pushing away from them. They both make a grab for my arm but I'm already out of their reach and spinning to face them.

"Why not?" Clint's almost pouting, and the sight of seeing this big, scary man *sad* breaks my heart, but I stick to my guns.

"Because I can't rely on you two! That's dangerous for me. I need to find my own footing. I'll be back at work tomorrow, I'll do extra shifts, I'll—"

"No!" Ezra bellows, his stool shrieking as he stands and pushes it back.

"What?" I shout, throwing my arms back. "What do you mean *no*?"

"I mean, *no*, you cannot go back there." He steps forward, grabbing my waist. "We'll provide for you, doll. We'll give you everything you need, want and more. You'll never have to work again, never reveal yourself for men who don't appreciate you again. We'd make sure you're always safe and *loved*, Aida. We can't live without you. We've waited long enough, you're not leaving us now!"

My heart swells at his possessive words and gaze, but it also makes me feel sick when his words *really* sink in.

"What do you mean 'waited long enough'?" I ask hesitantly, my body going stiff.

His face pales slightly, and I can feel Clint moving towards us. "Come on, you two, let's just talk—"

"What the *fuck* do you mean?" My teeth are clenched, my hands fisted at my side, my anxiousness turning to anger.

Ezra and Clint share a look and I swear I see *fear* on both of their faces.

"Aida, sweet, there's something we should probably admit to you."

I pull away from Ezra's grip but he doesn't let me go until Clint rests his hand on his best friend's shoulder and gives him a pointed look.

Only then does Ezra let go and I step back.

"Well?" I cock my hip and fold my arms, waiting expectantly, my heart racing.

"We watched you," Clint finally says, his voice low but still loud in my ears. "We watched you for two years. From afar after you caught our eye on the street. We've obsessed over you, Aida, and fallen in love with you at the same time."

My mouth opens and closes multiple times, my vision going slightly blurry as I lose focus. They *what*?

"You…you stalked me?"

My heart is racing in my ears as I stare at them, waiting for their answer.

And then, in unison like always, they nod.

But my stomach doesn't drop. My food doesn't come back up my throat. Nothing of the sort happens.

No, instead, I…*like* the idea of it. Of these two watching me, wanting me that badly when no one else did. *Loving* me, somehow.

But I don't voice that. I don't voice anything.

"Please, little doll," Ezra whispers, stepping forward. "We were going to tell you, I promise. But then you offered us a few days, and we wanted to win you over first. We can't just let you go, Aida."

I run what they've said over and over in my head, trying to make sense of everything, until I realise I don't want to.

I don't want to live on the streets.

I don't want to display my body for ungrateful men and sleazy bosses who don't care about my well being.

But none of that seems to matter in my mind—I just don't want to be without these two.

"So, what if I deny you? Say I'm leaving to my old job? What would you do?"

I wait as they look between each other, a silent conversation being spoken before me.

"I'd watch you from afar," Clint admits.

"I wouldn't let you go," Ezra shrugs.

214

I should be repulsed, but their openness to the truth and the fact they don't necessarily agree with each other draws me in instead.

Ezra just…wouldn't let me go? "You'd…kidnap me?" I whisper.

His lips tilt up in an amused smile he's attempting, and failing, to hold back. "Technically, it'd be abducting as you're not a kid, doll."

I roll my eyes but this time it's my turn to suppress a smile.

I can't help but eye the elevator keypad, and the both of them definitely notice. "Thinking of running, sweet girl?"

My heart races for a completely different reason at the idea, but I can't hide away with sex and denial. So instead, I take a step back and square my stance.

"So, you two have been stalking me, have fallen in love with me, and want me to move in with you and quit my job so you can care and dote on me for the rest of our lives?"

I expect them to laugh, to pull a face or

something. But no, they simply smile wide and nod, like I hit the fucking jackpot.

And I think I just might have.

TWELVE

 **EZRA**

How am I even supposed to focus when she's wearing that pretty little skirt and an even prettier, skimpier top?

"That's exactly what we want, sweetness," Clint agrees, but my eyes are zeroed in on where her arms are folded beneath her breasts.

When I flick my eyes up to look at the beauty of her face, I'm caught red handed. Her left eyebrow is raised, the look on her cute face unimpressed.

All I can do is shrug and shoot her a coy

smile. I'm immediately rewarded with her cheeks blushing a light pink.

But then she shakes her head and holds her hands out. "I just… How? How do you not understand that this all seems so fucking insane right now?"

She gets so in her own head.

"Because we're already obsessed with you, baby. We've been obsessed for two years."

"And we're done fucking waiting," I seethe, quickly stepping forward to wrap my arm around her waist and drag her against my body. She yelps, and places her hands against my chest to steady herself as if I won't always do that for her. "I'm an impatient man, Aida, and now I've had a taste, I can never let you go."

She doesn't fight when I grip the back of her head and crash my mouth onto hers. She doesn't fight when I nip her bottom lip and groan into her mouth. She doesn't fight when Clint steps behind her and cages her between us.

No, she fucking *adores* it. She whimpers

and moans and takes everything I give her with abandon.

Because she's my fucking girl, and no one will ever be able to take her away from me again.

"You'll stay with us, won't you, baby?" Clint whispers in her ear, skimming his hands over her body like he can't keep them in one place. I know exactly how he feels, she's perfect and I want to feel every piece of her. "Make us the happiest men alive?"

She moans when I nip at her neck, clamping my teeth around her skin lightly.

"Wh-what if you get bored of me and leave me with nothing?"

"Not going to fucking happen." I grab her face between my hands as Clint continues working his lips over her neck and back. "Even if *somehow* we didn't work out, you'd be leaving us with a place to stay and a heavy bank account. But know this—" I wrap her hair around my fist and tug back so she's forced to look at my face.

"You are *never* leaving us."

It doesn't take long to rip off our clothes, and as soon as they're gone, I have her bent over the island, Clint coming around the other side with a smirk on his face matching mine.

"You look so beautiful splayed out for us," he sighs, brushing her hair from her face as he looks down at her.

She's laid flat on the countertop, her legs hanging down in front of me and her head directly in line with Clint's cock.

"The best damned meal I've ever had." I lower to my knees and revel in the high-pitched sound of pleasure and surprise she makes as I dip my fingers in and spread her pretty cunt apart. She's dripping wet like always, her thighs smeared in a light coating of her want.

I wrap my hands around her thighs and lick up her sweet slit, teasing my tongue barely into her hole. Her moans turn muffled, and no doubt Clint has shoved his cock between her lips.

She writhes beneath my mouth, her sensitive

clit swollen with need.

It doesn't take long before she's crying out and shaking beneath me, her cum flooding my mouth like the most amazing drink.

I stand back up as her body goes limp, Clint's head hanging back as he groans and continues to fuck her mouth. She's looking up at him like he hung the moon, her body spent after only one orgasm.

It's a beautiful sight, but I've got more I want to do with her tight body.

I tease my hands gently over the backs of her thighs, over her ass and up the length of her back before returning to her thighs. I place my hands on the outside of them, pressing them tightly together.

My cock is rock hard, jutting out straight. I groan out loudly as I slip between the soft flesh of her thighs, slick with my saliva and her cum. She mewls as my thick length strokes her cunt with every stroke.

"So fucking beautiful." I pull back and

SEEKING AIDA

thrust back in, her warm skin hugging my cock perfectly. "You understand that, baby? You understand what you've done to us?"

"She's goddamned bewitched us." Clint grabs the sides of her face and thrusts forward quickly, fucking her mouth quicker and harder to match the pace I fuck her thighs. "Our perfect little girl has us wrapped around her finger."

"She feels so fucking good, Clint, and I'm not even in her tight pussy."

"Because she's perfect, our perfect little slut."

As soon as those words leave his lips, I feel her legs clamp harder around my cock, her body shaking as her second orgasm overtakes her.

"Fuck," Clint shouts, his thrusts going sloppy as he fills her mouth with his cum.

It's an erotic sight that sends me over the edge, her soft, tight thighs and the feel of her clit forcing my cum from my cock to coat the edge of the island and her skin.

I groan out my release, my heart feeling

fuller than before as acceptance settles over the three of us.

She's ours, and we're hers. We'd die for her, we'd do anything for her, when all she wants is for us to love her wholeheartedly.

And we do, we really fucking do.

EPILOGUE

Aida

"**F**uck, Aida, *fuck*."

My pussy grows wetter as I lean against the door, my ear pressed to the wood as I try and get as close as possible, needing to hear more.

They do this sometimes. They're so needy that me being away for even a few hours is too long for them.

I've been at the gym all evening, my skin now covered in sweat. Of course, not the public gym. No, they had one built so I didn't even have to leave the building, but they know how overwhelmed I can sometimes get, so they do give me my privacy. And they always know when I want it.

But right now, all I want is to see what is no doubt incredibly hot.

The first time I'd caught them doing this, I almost came in my panties just watching them.

I wrap my hand around the handle and push slowly, not wanting to alert them of my presence just yet.

Clint is standing behind Ezra, the both of them dressed in only a pair of low-slung joggers. One arm is wrapped around Ezra's waist, his free hand wrapped around his best friend's cock.

Ezra's always been the needier of the two. This big, scary man is the complete opposite inside. His face is that of pure bliss as he thrusts into Clinton's hand who's cock is no doubt digging into his back.

They've never stepped over this line of hand jobs, but maybe one day I'll get to see more.

"Are you thinking of those little black shorts she left in? The ones you got her because they barely cover her ass?" Ezra nods eagerly, his eyes closed. "God, I think about taking that cunt every second of every day. You need her, don't you? You need her to take all your cum into her pussy so you can fill her up."

When I move my eyes from Ezra's, Clint is staring directly at me, a sly smirk on his face.

"Open your eyes, Ezzie," he murmurs, and as soon as Ezra's gaze connects with mine, he grunts, white ropes of cum shooting out into Clint's hand.

"Aida," he sighs, Clint slowing his strokes to draw out all the cum he can. "You're back."

His smile is lazy as he moves away from Clint to dart forward and wrap me up in a hug. "I missed you, baby," he murmurs, rapidly kissing me over my head and face.

I laugh and light heartedly try to push him away, not that he'd ever let me. I hear the tap running beside us, and not long later Clint is behind me, wrapping me in his own arms.

"How was your workout, sweet girl?"

"It was good," I smile, still on an energetic high. I'm jumpy, and after viewing one of my boyfriends fuck my other boyfriends fist? Even more so.

"Look at her, bouncing around like that," Clint chuckles, his hands palming my breasts, his cock digging into my lower back. "You still got energy, sweetness?"

I nod eagerly, my lips parting as Ezra's begin to make light kisses down my neck. "Lots and lots," I pant.

They both chuckle. "Is that so?" Ezra murmurs. "I think there's only one way to get rid of that."

I hum my agreement, but squeal in shock when I'm lifted by a pair of hands at my sides. Immediately, I wrap my legs around Ezra's waist and my arms around his neck.

"You ready to go again?" I question, as if I don't already know the answer. Everyday, I'm fucked by the both of them—sometimes at the same time—at least once, and that's a very rare minimum. And Gods do I know how many times they can go.

Clint laughs from behind us as Ezra huffs. "You questioning me, little girl?"

I'm about to answer with something snarky but my voice is cut off when I'm hauled backwards to land on what I immediately register as my bed.

Ever since I agreed to stay with them, they've made what was the spare—and then mine—room all of ours. Sure, it's filled with my things and decorated as I want it to be, but they practically live here with me.

And I know Clinton particularly likes my jasmine scented candles, and Ezra the fluffy pink comforter.

"I asked you a question," Ezra says calmly, way too calmly for my liking, as he stands at the bottom of the bed with his hands on his hips.

"*You questioning me, little boy?*" I mimic

back, using my hand to make a chatting motion.

I see—and feel—the results of my tone immediately.

His eyes gleam like they always do when I bicker, and with ease, he reaches down to wrap a hand around my ankle, tugging me to the bottom of the bed.

He flips me over, an arm under my stomach to lift my ass up in the air like a presentation.

"That fucking mouth," he spits, his hands circling my ass. A second later, one comes down, connecting with the soft flesh. I cry out and bury my face into the sheets. "I think it needs occupying."

I know what he means even before I feel the bed dip as Clint positions himself in front of me, even before he wraps my hair around his fist and yanks back, and even before I'm presented with one of my favourite things in the world.

Ezra brings his hand down on me again just as Clint surges forward and buries his cock in my mouth.

"Atta girl," he groans, tipping his head back as I hollow out my cheeks and suck him like my life depends on it.

I'm so lost in the sensation of pleasing this man that I almost jump when a new one is added to my dripping wet cunt. Something firm but soft circles my hole, and then my clit, before slipping an inch back into my pussy.

"You ready, baby?"

I nod, a very restricted action, and clamp my eyes shut as Ezra begins to slip the vibrator further inside of me. "Fuck, she looks so good taking it."

"Shut up or I'll blow," Clint groans, the words making me suck harder and bob my head faster. Although my attempts are for naught when he pulls out quick enough he needs to balance me. "Naughty," he mutters, tracing the tip over my wet lips. "You think that was a smart move?"

It doesn't matter what I think because all coherent thoughts leave my body when the toy inside of me begins to vibrate, my back bowing in pure pleasure.

"That's it, doll. How does it feel?" It's not as though I can answer until he turns it off with the remote, and I'm whining out in protest.

The both of them laugh like it's the most entertaining thing in the world to watch me writhe beneath them, and then it's back on.

I can feel my orgasm begin to build rapidly as the world around me fades, but before I can feel that glorious high, I'm stripped of my stimulation with the click of a button.

"You thought it was going to be that easy, sweet thing?" Clint murmurs as Ezra begins to kiss up my back. "Aww, poor girl. You really did, didn't you?"

I snap my head up and narrow my eyes at him, adoring the devilish tint to his handsome face as he stares right back down at me, consumed by lust.

"If you're not going to fuck me," I grumble, rolling over onto my back and sitting up, but before I can move off the bed, I'm tugged back by hands under my armpits.

"What a silly thing to say," Clint whispers into my ear as Ezra moves forwards on his knees, hands sliding up my calves. "Think she deserves to be fucked like a dirty little slut?"

Ezra looks as though he's seriously considering that question as he pulls my legs apart, Clint still holding me up by the arms like I'm some sort of offering. The toy moves slightly inside of me as Ezzie shifts my legs onto his shoulders, and I'm hoisted in the air between them.

"She hasn't earned it yet." He removes one hand from my leg to the bed, reaching for something, and then I realise what when the vibrator is turned on and my spine arches.

They keep me hoisted between them, watching me with rapt attention as I succumb to the intense pleasure. But it's not enough, because it's not them.

"There we go," Ezra sighs, massaging my calf on top of his shoulder as I feel my body begin to shake. "Let's see you come for us, little doll."

Clint lowers me so I'm lying on his lap, smiling down at me as Ezra keeps my legs in the air, so I'm hanging half upside down. Clint strokes my hair and offers me sweet praise as Ezra stares at my cunt hungrily, watching as his toy wrings out everything I have.

"Well done, baby, we're so proud of you. One orgasm and then we'll fill you up with our cum. How does that sound, hmm?"

It sounds fucking perfect, proven when not even a second later, I'm shaking in their arms and clamping my eyes shut as an orgasm wracks over my body.

"That's my girl," Clint repeats, stroking the T-zone of my forehead over and over as I come down to earth, but only mentally as Ezra still has me hoisted half up in the air.

I twitch as he pulls out the toy, placing it beside him. "She did such a good job, didn't she?" he asks his best friend, who nods with a grin. I give them both a lazy smile knowing that we're nowhere near over.

He slides my legs down to his waist. I somehow find it in me to hook them around him. "Fuck," he groans, tracing his tip over my clit. "She's fucking soaked, Clint. Covered in her own cum."

"Fill her with yours," Clint chuckles, still playing with my hair. "Mark her, make sure everyone knows she's ours."

"Gladly." And with that, he thrusts inside of me, filling me up instantly. I claw at the bedsheets as he grips my ass, fucking into me like I'm his world.

And I know I am.

Our bodies come together perfectly like always. I adore the way mine responds to his and his to mine after a year of being taken care of, loved and cherished like I hung the moon.

"Perfect, perfect girl." He wraps his hands around my waist, our skin slapping together as his pace speeds up and I feel myself near my second orgasm. "That's it, baby, you're so tight. You feel like heaven."

"You look so beautiful like this," Clint whispers, his fingers teasing light strokes around my nipples. "Does he feel good, sweetheart?"

I nod aimlessly, unable to focus as my legs start to shake and tighten around Ezra's waist. His hands squeeze my waist protectively and the small, barely noticeable sensation sets me off.

I throw my hands back aimlessly, grabbing at Clinton's chest as pleasure overwhelms me and I tighten around Ezra's cock. He groans, a beautiful noise that makes my skin tingle, and pumps into me with three unfocused thrusts before I feel his cum coat my insides.

"Such a pretty girl, taking all his cum. We're so proud of you."

My smile feels right as Ezra pulls out and lowers me carefully. Clint immediately turns me so I'm straddling him with our chests pressed together. He pulls me close, taking all my weight.

"How are you feeling, baby?" His hard cock

rubs against my clit, betraying my sweet man's kindness for what he really feels.

"Perfect," I manage to mumble.

It hasn't been the easiest year but it's still been utter perfection from the get go. It took me a while to get used to relying on these two men, but as soon as I adjusted to the princess lifestyle, it was beautiful. I'd always thought relying on people was dangerous, but I was wrong.

Still, the passwords to the security systems have all been changed to ones I've picked special to me, my savings account only I have access to is filled, and I now have passports and solid paperwork. These men—well, only Clint seeing as Ezra repeats how he'd keep me locked up as his sex pet every chance he gets—have done everything they can to reassure me, and I've felt nothing but safe since.

The tip of his cock traces my clit as he teases me, scanning my face with heated eyes like he hasn't already ingrained my face into his mind.

"Our precious thing," he whispers,

reminding me of the fact I belong to them before surging up and inside of me. The motion doesn't surprise me, but my body treats it as though his thick cock is a new sensation, begging to fit around him.

"That's it," he mutters, holding me close as he uses his hold on me to bring us together again. "No matter how many times I feel this perfect pussy, it blows my mind every fucking time."

Pleasure courses through my body as he takes me harder and harder, my breaths turning into cut-off pants as I struggle to get oxygen in. Everything's hazy outside of us, my mind completely focused on the man before me as he continues to give me everything he has.

Mind, body and soul.

'You feel so good,' is what I try to say, but it comes out as, "Good-nghh…feel…good."

My body barely warns me when I'm smacked by my third orgasm, clenching hard around Clinton's cock as he fucks me faster.

"Oh fuck, yes baby, squeeze me just like

that. Holy *fu*—" He throws his head back, pulling me down hard onto him as he groans out my name and fills me full of his cum that's no doubt mixing with Ezra's.

The thought and the feel of the warm liquid coating my insides drags out my orgasm until I'm using Clint's body to hold up my own, twitching against him.

He shuffles back so he can lean against the headboard, his arms coming around my waist to hold me close. After a moment of silence, he swipes my hair back from my face to plant a soft kiss on my forehead.

I feel the bed dip as Ezra—now dressed in grey joggers and holding a glass of ice-cold water—moves to lay beside us.

"Thank you," I mumble, letting him press the glass to my lips. A few drops spill out as I greedily chug the water.

He places the glass back down and Clint lifts me off of him, a mixture of all our cum dripping out of me. They both groan at the sight, but I laugh and snuggle between them, shaking my head.

"Nu-uh, remove your mind from the gutter, boys. Your girl is completely worn out."

"My girl," Ezra sighs lovingly, his eyes going gooey as he drags me closer towards him.

"*Ours*," Clinton repeats possessively, wrapping an arm around both of our waists to keep me squashed between them.

Peace and calm washes over me completely. My fear of being abandoned never returns, nor does the need to pull away or protect myself.

It hasn't come back for some time and I know it won't ever need to again.

I'm safe, loved, and protected. As well as thoroughly fucked.

It's now I realise I haven't once thought about my devastating excuse of a family, and especially not my disappearing act of a father.

There's no need, not when I'm finally happy.

"Yours."

Thank you!

Thank you for reading 'Seeking Aida', I hope you enjoyed her story! If you did, be sure to check out my socials for news on this series and more, as well as additional bonus content! Or even check out my website for regular updates and info!

www.agloewwrites.co.uk

A. G. Loew's Socials:

Email:
agloew.writes@gmail.com

Instagram, TikTok & Twitter:
@agloew_writes

Support?

Leaving a review on online seriously helps us authors out – and it's free! I appreciate this more than I can put into words, and love reading the feedback I receive.

Better yet, check out my Patreon!

Printed in Great Britain
by Amazon